Curse of the Blacknoc Witch

by

Tori V. Rainn

This is a work of fiction. Names, characters, places, and incidents are either the product of the author's imagination or are used fictitiously, and any resemblance to actual persons living or dead, business establishments, events, or locales, is entirely coincidental.

Curse of the Blacknoc Witch

Contact Information: info@thewildrosepress.com

Cover Art by *Abigail Owen*

The Wild Rose Press, Inc.
PO Box 708
Adams Basin, NY 14410-0708
Visit us at www.thewildrosepress.com

Publishing History
First Mainstream Fantasy Rose Edition, 2020
Print ISBN 978-1-5092-3087-7
Digital ISBN 978-1-5092-3088-4

Published in the United States of America

The thick tree canopy shields me from the bright stars. Lucky for me, I see well at night. All monsters do.

Two swift monsters dash between trees like rabid wolves. I am the second one, just behind the monster pursuing the boy. I put an end to the monster's hunt when I corner the ugly beast at the dense brush. Also enclosed in our cluster is the boy, who whimpers as he tries to slip through the branches only to snag his shirt sleeve on the sharp twigs. Before the beast can run after him, I stand in the way of its prey. I'm used to taking the same stance over and over, so it comes easy for me. Being a monster myself, there are some advantages I can always rely on. The primal instinct to keep fighting is one of them.

The beast charges me. I charge back. Our furry chests slam together on impact. Our claws dig slivers of skin off each other. I lose my grip on Ugly. I yank a vine off a tree and wrap it around Ugly's bulging neck. Seven feet of muscle thrashes against the restraint. The beast flashes his long canines as he claws and roars. I roar back, tugging on the vine once more. Ugly tosses a horned elbow into my stomach. I jam my horned head into his neck.

The vine snaps, and Ugly bolts.

I catch the monster's hind legs, my claws digging into his underfur of barbs.

Dedication

To my mom, my best friend, my rock.
You are the reason why
I grow into a better version of myself every day.

Dedication

[illegible]

[illegible]

[illegible]

Chapter One

To the young ones who fall and do wicked deeds:
The monsters will find you and pull you like weeds.
Roaming forever until you are dead.
Hunting together until they are fed.
But only through the darkest of hours.
Some may last before fate devours.
A nightmare repeats, but this is much worse.
You can't outrun the Blacknoc Curse.

I will never forget the night it came for me. The Blacknoc Curse.

The thick tree canopy shields me from the bright stars. Lucky for me, I see well at night. All monsters do.

Two swift monsters dash between trees like rabid wolves. I am the second one, just behind the monster pursuing the boy. I put an end to the monster's hunt when I corner the ugly beast at the dense brush. Also enclosed in our cluster is the boy, who whimpers as he tries to slip through the branches only to snag his shirt sleeve on the sharp twigs. Before the beast can run after him, I stand in the way of its prey. I'm used to taking the same stance over and over, so it comes easy for me. Being a monster myself, there are some advantages I can always rely on. The primal instinct to keep fighting is one of them.

The beast charges me. I charge back. Our furry chests slam together on impact. Our claws dig slivers of skin off each other. I lose my grip on Ugly. I yank a vine off a tree and wrap it around Ugly's bulging neck. Seven feet of muscle thrashes against the restraint. The beast flashes his long canines as he claws and roars. I roar back, tugging on the vine once more. Ugly tosses a horned elbow into my stomach. I jam my horned head into his neck.

The vine snaps, and Ugly bolts.

I catch the monster's hind legs, my claws digging into his underfur of barbs.

"Get out of here!" I yell at the boy. He stares blankly at me at first, and then pulls free from the brush and sprints away. I sigh. I often receive that look of confusion from the others. The humans. Maybe it shocks them because I'm the only freak who can speak. I barely understand it myself. Everything changed the moment I resisted the curse. Well, to some extent. I'm still hideous, fangs and all.

Ugly tears out of my grasp and bounds for the boy. On all fours, I sprint after Ugly, trying to match his agile speed as he gains on his next meal. I stop and point my claws at the brush between the boy and Ugly. The powers I wield emerged the day I went against the curse. My puffed chest burns, exhausting the last effort of my power. The brush rises and curls into a net, blocking the monster before it can clamp its teeth on the boy. He scurries away out of sight. Good boy.

Ugly turns to me, his teeth flashing and the barbs under his fur standing erect. I force a grin, even though I know it'll stoke the other monster's anger, and I'll pay for it. Like a disease on four muscular paws, the other beast scrambles back at me. The power I used to create the net has left me. I can't even lift an arm. With one swift move, Ugly's grimy claws tear through my stomach.

I crash to the ground, holding my wound and moaning.

Satisfaction warms me beneath the pain. The boy is free.

It was worth it.

Glassy, black eyes stare at me in disgust. This particular monster always fights me with extra malice because I don't chase and devour all the wicked children.

I foam at the mouth, snarling. "Not while I'm still here, Ugly."

Ugly eyes me with a death stare that conveys he isn't done with me. But then he growls and darts away, fixating on a new scent somewhere in the distance.

Once upon a time, *Ugly* was also a boy. His name was Josh. Nineteen, not much older than me. He was in the shed with me that day. If I had any say in it, the Blacknoc Curse should have come after him first. I guess it was only a matter of time before the curse came for us all.

When I had learned of Josh's wicked deed, the curse forced me to go after him. The flesh of the sister-abuser had tasted like black ash in my mouth. When I ate him, and then vomited him back out, he was no longer a boy, but a monster just like the rest out here—lean and muscular with powerful claws, gray skin laden with needle-like fur, and a narrow-wrinkled snout packing rows of pointy teeth.

As Josh disappears among the dense forest, I am

left alone, slumped by a tree. No one can escape this forest realm. It's a supernatural void no one can see. Nothing like the one I lived in back home with Pa. It's true hell. Why I choose to save the kids each night is beyond me. They'll just get thrown back into this forest. How long has it been like this? Three years since my curse? Three unbelievable years since I've seen Pa, since I've seen anything else but this evil forest. And only a month since I've been saving kids from the jaws of those beasts, from becoming monsters like myself.

I'm deceiving myself. Saving the kids won't break the Blacknoc Curse. It won't change me. It will never stop.

I cringe, bending down on all fours.

In the distance, the shrieks of a girl rattle the night air. I shoot up and the wrenching pain in my belly almost topples me. I've never heard a girl out here before.

Groaning through gritted teeth, I push up again and try to steady myself as my torn flesh heals itself. If there's one thing the Blacknoc Curse is good for, it's a speedy recovery.

Another girlish shriek echoes through the woods. My ears pick up rapid panting. Small footfalls. Following that is heavy paws. Deep animal breathing through thick nostrils. Dread twists my gut. I know what those things will do to her. The same thing they do to every other kid out here—chew them up then vomit them out into a beast.

As I lean against the tree, part of me can't help but wonder what she did. Then I curse. What she did is of no importance to me. She could have killed her own father for all I cared. No one deserves to become this wretched…*thing,* trapped in this hellhole forever.

My gashes close to slits.

Shoving forward, I follow the feminine aroma of sweat and fear. I glimpse her raggedy cloak, fluttering around a tree as she tries to lose the snarling brute behind her. But its powerful snout is not dumb enough to miss her pungent scent. Those stubby, erect ears aren't distracted enough to miss her panicked breathing.

With a flick of my wrist, I launch a spurt of ghostly white energy across the forest to smack into the brush opposite the girl.

The monster takes the bait and investigates the noise. *Stupid.*

I search for the girl on the other side of the tree. Her long black hair competes with the night sky. The moment her brown eyes meet mine, her scream vibrates my eardrums.

I try to mash my paw across her trembling lips, but she scrambles back.

"Stop it," I whisper. "They're sensitive to sound. Let me help you." Never using it much, I can't imagine what the sound of my voice sounds like to a human. Probably gruff, like a demon swallowing sheets of bark.

The girl is young. Must be around seventeen, a year younger than me. She slaps at my barbed covered hands, only to prick herself. The drops of blood on her skin provoke me to snap at the liquid for a taste. I reach for a single red drop with my paw before it can hit the ground. Bringing the blood to my snout, I lick it. The taste of putrid sin swarms my mind. Her wickedness. Whatever she did, it's bad. I growl, taking a step back. But her sin can never be as bad as what I did.

Holding her hand, the girl's lower lip quivers.

I shove back the urge to apologize for hurting her. For scaring her. I can't help how I look. My appearance resembles the other killing maniacs, so why should I expect her to go anywhere with me?

A monster plows through the undergrowth. I stifle a growl. The girl's scent is hard to miss and could attract more beasts.

Stepping between her and the approaching paws, I extend my claws. "Get out of here. Go!"

I whirl in time to tackle the charging beast against a tree. The tree bends on impact. The other monster's jaw snaps under my arm. It launches me across a clearing. I crash onto the dirt.

Somewhere else in the forest, a familiar scream erupts. It's the boy I saved earlier. I punch the dirt and push to my feet. As strong and fast as I am, I can't save them all. I flex my claws. How can I stop the monsters from creating more monsters?

The girl's thrumming heartbeat catches my attention. Without thinking, I sprint toward her, dashing through the trees like a wild dog. I want to keep her heart beating as long as possible.

The hem of her cloak vanishes behind a foliage-covered mound. Beyond that the sun is rising. Relief floods me. She's safe, for now. The Blacknoc Curse will toss her back to her home from where it snatched her. But like always, the curse will return tonight for the missing sinners. It will come for them every night until their punishment is fulfilled.

I stop to catch my breath. My throat tightens. I force myself to take a deep breath and release it. Eventually, I'll slip up and won't be there in time to protect them. The kids will be chomped into pieces, then spit out as furry minions. I expel a roar. What is the point of trying to stop the cycle? Maybe because I can grant them the opportunity to return home each morning? It's not much, but at least they have that. A transformed monster like myself can't leave the forest. I often wonder if it's because my soul is dead. I can't even remember the last time I heard my pulse. Do I even have a heart anymore?

Rage crashes through me, ready to unleash. I take it out on a nearby tree, carving up the bark until splinters make my paw bleed.

"When does it stop?" I grumble.

The sun creeping through the tree canopy singes me. With a hiss I dissolve into the dirt, as if it's my grave. Here, I sleep until I rise tonight for another hunt. Another opportunity to protect them.

Chapter Two

The moonlight gleams along the forest floor tonight. Good. It'll make it easier for the kids to see as they flee the beasts. I remember what it's like to run from such hideous creatures. I wonder how many of them regret the decision that led them here. I regret my own every day. And every day the memory replays like a bad dream.

Nobody saw us that day in the dilapidated shed. Pa probably would've whipped me bloody in front of the entire village if he'd witness what I'd done. When the boys kept shouting at me to do it, I gave into the pressure before they taunted me.

My throat swells as the image of my doing resurfaces.

What a fool I was to think an initiation could earn their acceptance. But that was a long time ago. I'm far from the normal life I dreamed of escaping, and now wished I'd accepted. I brush the past aside. None of that matters anymore. It doesn't change what I am.

Monsters rustle along the ground, like a pack of demented bears hungry for their next course. Since my decision to resist eating children, they have disowned me. They even tried to kill me when I first committed to protecting the kids. But a monster can't just kill another monster—we heal too fast, and the Blacknoc Curse basically makes all monsters immortal. But that doesn't stop them from slitting my throat each chance they get.

A breeze ruffles the leaves. I smell sweat, mixed with adrenaline induced by stress. The humans. They've arrived. Against their will, the curse has once again plucked the sinners from their beds and thrown them into this unearthly forest like teleportation magic from hell. I'm prolonging their fate. This I know. They all become monsters in the end. But I can't just sit back and watch them become beasts. I must follow my conscience and pursue the chance to save them.

The monsters scatter. The hunt starts.

Ear-splitting screams erupt, and I'm torn between which to follow. There is one not a part of this group of screams. One that makes little to no noise. I must rely on my snout. A distinct smell fills my nostrils. The aroma reminds me of autumn. The girl. I inhale her faint scent. It barely reaches me, and then it's gone. The wind fails me this time.

Standing perfectly still, I concentrate on her footfalls on the dirt, like a frightened heartbeat.

Trying to ignore the chaos breaking out around me, I pinpoint a location half a mile away. Her autumn aroma confirms I'm close.

Using each tree as shelter, I sneak up on the girl. She's crouched over something. I narrow my eyes. She's sharpening the edge of a stick against a rock. It's a fair-sized spear long enough to pin me to a tree. *Impressive.*

This girl is a survivor.

I dare to step into her hidden territory.

Leaping up, she raises her spear toward me, ready to launch it. Her earthy brown eyes widen.

"Hello." My greeting sounds stupid, but it's the

only thing in my head besides her aroma.

"Y-you? The one who told me to run?" She shakes her head. "I'm going insane. A Blacknoc monster protecting me? That's impossible."

"No, it's not. I didn't eat you, did I?" I inch closer to her. Her knuckles whiten as she grips the spear harder. "As you can see, I'm not exactly like them."

"How can you sound almost…human? What are you?"

I shrug my thorny shoulders.

Twigs snap and break in the distance. Fear pulses through me. "We need to keep moving. You can't stay in the same spot. They will always track you."

I reach to grip her hand, but she pulls away.

"Why are you helping me?"

I check over her shoulder, then bring my gaze back on hers. "If you keep asking questions, you're going to get eaten. Let's go."

Her lips part. She gives a slight nod.

"Stay with me."

I dash and zip through the trees, but her tiny footfalls grow faint. I twist around. She is running, exhausted, and barely catching up. More tree limbs break closer this time. She's too slow.

She meets me, her breathing rapid and cheeks flushed. "Slow down."

"We can't." I glance at her dark, slender body under her haggard cloak. She stares up at me. For a girl, she's tall. Five-nine probably. At seven feet in monster height on two hind legs, I easily tower over her. Her thick, expressive brows raise in question. I eye the cloak again. "Take that off."

She grabs the clasp. "Why?"

"Decoy. Monsters are sensitive to smell."

She grips the cloak tight, clenches her jaw, and then finally hands it to me. Like the moment before rain hits the dirt, I want to inhale her autumn scent but resist shoving it into my snout. There is a nature about her I can't ignore.

I motion toward a tree and glance up. I could use my powers to lower a branch and hook the cloak, but it's not worth the weakening that results. My strength may be needed elsewhere. Besides, I have other useful skills. Like a feline, I claw up the tree until I'm at the top and fasten the cloak as a silhouette on a branch. It should slow them down for the time being.

Skidding along the bark, I hurry back down. Her eyes are wide, her mouth gaping. I can't tell if she's impressed or horrified at how fast I am on my paws.

As we run, the piercing screams of the other children echo around us, their last pleas grating my skull. Guilt drowns my chest.

"We have to keep them safe," the girl says.

She stops. When I turn, her pleading eyes drill a stake through my chest. I'm surprised by her selflessness. What did she do to deserve the Blacknoc Curse?

"We can't save them all," I mutter.

"But you're helping me."

For now. Her fate is inevitable, and I am still fighting that fact. "We have to keep moving."

She trips over a branch. I bend to grab her hand to help her up, but she shrieks in my grasp.

The girl yanks away, bloody pricks on her hand.

Stupid. How can I forget?

"I'm so sorry. I didn't mean to hurt you."

But I couldn't help it either. Layers of torment cover my body. Small barbs protrude out of every inch of my skin, and that's just my sub layer of fur. Short horns stick out from my elbows, and skull—even one on my chin. Everything I touch I damage.

"You need to stop the blood," I urge. "They'll smell it. And keep running."

Tracking the direction of the wind, I try my best to guide her into hiding. Glancing over my shoulder, I watch her struggling to keep up.

The girl winces and wraps her hand with a cloth she tore from the bottom of her shirt. Half of her slim belly is exposed. I'd almost forgotten what it feels like to look at a girl. Her rich brown skin must be smooth and warm to the touch. I'd forgotten what it feels like to have skin, too.

"I'm sorry," I say again, almost in a whisper.

She straightens, her hands trembling slightly. "I suppose you can't help what you are."

Somehow, her words are sharper than my claws. Holding back a fit of rage takes every ounce of my mental strength. If I was human, I would have never hurt her. Without a word, I guide the way, and she follows reluctantly.

Taking paths I know will mask her scent, I put distance between us and the fading screams. I glance at her trekking behind. Her hands clasp her arms. I don't even know her name, or why she's here.

Her shallow breathing pounds my ears. "Can't we just run home? I am sure my house is this way."

"There is no going home." The words char my tongue. "That's part of the curse. It won't let you escape. You will return to this place every night again and again, until…"

She slumps to the ground, and her breathing increases. Not only does she emit too much noise, but I fear she might hyperventilate. I can't blame her. I've learned the hard way there is no way out of this nightmare-fest forest. When I was human like her, I gave up and stopped running. That's just what happens when hope runs out.

I crouch down next to the girl, careful not to touch her. "Look. You'll be okay as long as you stay with me."

She sniffles and cups her face. "This can't be happening." She wipes a tear off her cheek. "The legend of the curse is really like what my great-aunt said."

I stand and pace. My monster self cannot be still when on constant alert. "It's all true. A real cesspool of teeth."

"When I woke back in my room, the scratches on my skin from last night were still there. Grandfather thought I'd done it to myself. I told him what happened, and he didn't believe me."

"He won't be able to help anyway."

She moans, and I stifle a grunt. There I go again with my optimism. As long as I am cursed to this flesh, there just isn't any room for the stuff. But I can't avoid the truth of her fate.

I kneel to her level. "What's your name?"

"Layla Marlowe."

I smile. A fitting name for a gorgeous girl. "Layla," I repeat, as if the name carries me back to a reality where humans live in harmony away from monsters. I hurriedly add, "Nice to meet you." Then I remember our situation. My comment is inappropriate. There's nothing nice about the forest. Social etiquette must have died along with my soul.

"And you?" She looks up at me with a curious gaze. "Do you have a name?"

It's been so long since I've heard my name. Who said it last? Josh? Pa calling me to supper? I stop to think for a second and then allow it to roll off my tongue.

"Samuel Fawcett."

She hugs her knees, leaning forward, dangerously near my barbed hands. "What a keen name for a monster."

An odd musk from between the trees reaches me. The stench of fear grows potent as low branches snap. Someone small and clumsy runs toward us.

I leap up. "We need to go now."

"No. I can't run anymore."

"Please, Layla. Go."

She studies me, lips parted. Before I can assure her of safety, feet stomp on the crunchy foliage. I reel to meet a boy racing between the trees. Behind him are two sprinting monsters, ready to pounce.

The boy freezes before slamming into me. I shove him out of the way, hurting him, and launch myself at both snarling beasts. Nitwit and Slobber, I'll call them. My arm finds the nearest neck and wraps around Nitwit. My jaw clamps around the shoulder of Slobber like it's a raging dog, itching to chomp down on the panicked kids.

The boy and Layla scramble back in horror. I won't be able to entertain the monsters much longer before they free themselves and dart off after my comrades. I need a little help.

I focus on the vines near Layla's ankles and expel my energy. The boy and Layla gasp as vines grow up and curve every which way, wrapping them into a thorny cage. A few purple flowers even blossom from the vines. That is new.

My arms go weak. Slobber wiggles out of my grasp and races toward the vine-cage. Layla and the boy shriek as Slobber slams snout first into the enclosure. The monster wails on impact and tries another tactic, clawing at the structure.

Nitwit wrestles me to the ground, ramming my back with its head horns. I roar. A horned elbow stabs into me and pain explodes in my hip. A thick jaw full of razor teeth clamps around my leg and gives it a gut-wrenching shake.

I yelp as I pry its mouth away with the last of my strength. The sharp spines on my leg bend back and break. Some even stick in Nitwit's mouth, bloodying it.

Slobber remains clawing at the cage. Thorny vines snap and creak. The cage won't hold much longer. Her face wet with tears, Layla shields the boy with her arms and body in the far corner like a momma protecting her cub. She doesn't even know that boy yet protects him.

Lifted by her defiant spirit, I try to stand. But Nitwit goes for my neck and clamps down, giving it a good shake before going back to my wounded leg. Satisfied with the damage, Nitwit drops my bloody, twisted limb and joins its friend.

"Stay back!" The fear in Layla's tone sinks its hook into me.

I scramble on all fours like I used to when I ate kids, floppy leg and all, and charge the beasts. My body slams into theirs, and they yelp against the cage.

Another snap in the vines reverberates.

I tackle the monsters repeatedly. Punches and kicks. Anything to keep their attention on me.

A shy ray of sunlight pokes through the tree canopy. The monsters hiss and dart away into the shadows. I glance back at the dented cage. Streaks of sunlight quickly fall on it, and I step back. Before it's time to disappear, I take one last look at Layla.

"Wait. Come back," she shouts. "Are you okay?"

Her concern stuns me. Shifting back, and forth, she struggles to find me in the shadows. As much I want to run to her and inspect her for wounds, I can't. Not while I'm bound to this sick curse. As I sink into the earthlike mist, the cage crumbles and falls to the ground.

Chapter Three

Grandfather's snoring in the next room. The small cottage allows such noises to escape. I'm wide awake and can't sleep anymore. After the last two nights, I can barely rest for fear of waking up back in that forest. Is it even a real forest? It didn't feel like it, but like another world birthing darkness. Certainly not of this earth.

Sitting on the cushioned bench, I lean into the morning sun shining through the window and twirl the purple flower between my fingers.

His name is Samuel, and he saved my life. Twice.

Why would a monster save me? Fight for me? That beast didn't even know me, or what I'd done.

I creep out of my room and glance through the gap of Grandfather's bedroom door. He's all I have. The only man who would break his knuckles for me. Yet, he doesn't believe me about the forest. I showed him the marks on my hands. Even after flashing the proof he thinks I speak lies. He thinks I'm covering the truth with a tall tale. Maybe Samuel is right. No one can help.

My grip tightens around the purple flower. No. That's not possible! There must be a way out of this mess.

As quietly as possible, I hurry to pack a basket of food. I leave a note on the table saying I will be at the library in Grutchburg City and will return as soon as I can. A part of me prays I will return in time to see Grandfather.

I dig in my armoire for a cloak. It drapes over me as I dash out the door, careful to close it so as not to wake Grandfather.

With the curse counting down my minutes, I quickly mount my horse and trot for three hours until I reach the library in Grutchburg City outside my village. By the time I make it to the city, sweat drenches my back. Grutchburg City is a smaller city compared to Rydmont City. Its wide avenues and orderly buildings make up for its lack of vibrant colors. The streets are quiet. Few people walk about. Most stay home. Others go about their business in and out of markets and taverns.

My boots click up the library steps. Between the pillars, I push open the double doors with the letters G and L etched on each door.

A design of a massive sparrow gliding over a stream fills the stone floor. The circular lobby is lined with a few benches. Seats are occupied by readers. Outside of that, rows and rows of bookshelves hint of paths. Some lead to more secluded reading rooms. Other paths follow the spiraling stairs across a long balcony full of even more bookshelves.

I head toward the sign in the back that says LEGENDS AND MYTHS. Usually, adolescents roam this room, but today I'm lucky to be alone. The dim candles flickering on the walls and reading tables add to the shivers in my spine.

The Blacknoc book I came for is nowhere to be found. Did I imagine it? When I mention it to the librarian, he has no idea of its whereabouts and claims it went missing months ago. I resort to searching through other books for help.

My candle melts down to its wick. I must retrieve another light to finish my fifth book. The whole day wasted reading about curses and how to repel witches. As if an herb tea would break my spell.

As I move back to the bookshelf to return the book, a black rectangle behind the rows of books catches my attention. I pull out the books to unveil the shadow.

Covered in dust and cobwebs is the Blacknoc book. Of course, it would hide in the shadows, as if the library itself exiled the curse's atrocious nature.

I grab the book and clean it with my sleeve. I'm familiar with the legendary story. Everyone who listened to their parents' bedtime stories has heard of the Blacknoc Curse.

Pulling up a chair, I slam the book on the table.

The Blacknoc Curse is written in red on the black leather-bound tome. Its silver border glistens. In the center of the book is a design of a witch's knot. The corners are worn, as if it has been dropped one too many times.

I skim the first few pages. No words, but weird illustrations that seem to mean nothing at times but allude to the curse. Abstract drawings of deformed, monster-like faces chasing what I can only assume are children. The final pages are practically filled with depictions of hands surfacing from a lake of blood.

The images seem to induce every effect except the helpful kind. A throb begins to work its way into my head. There must be a clue on how to break the curse. I have to look carefully at the pictures.

While eating my sandwich, I guide the lantern over

a page. The pictures depict the same old story of a witch giving birth to her only son. She leaves her infant boy in her cottage for only a few minutes to fetch water in the stream. When she returns, her house is ablaze. Her son can't be heard crying.

I gag at the drawing of a burnt baby and turn away. Mr. Alden, the librarian, passes by the room and arches a brow at me. Ignoring him, I force myself back to the grisly image and quickly flip to the next page.

The witch later learns of two boys bragging about how they had snuck into her home to steal from her. They admitted to not seeing a baby inside when they lit the curtains on fire. The witch demanded justice and reported the murderers. But the law only saw one criminal—her. For practicing witchcraft, she was burnt at the stake, but not before she punished the boys who'd taken her son.

A drawing depicts the witch with black eyes and dendritic veins along the side of her face. Wailing and screaming at the sky, she'd unleashed a power like no other, cursing children who committed true acts of wickedness to be hunted, eaten, and transformed into monsters.

Samuel's appearance flashes across my mind. Fangs. Claws that shred. A face that could scare the shadows away. I cringe, trying to block out the truth of what he is. Am I any different?

Written in cursive beneath the witch illustration is, *"Turned inside out into their true natures."*

A picture of two monsters resembles the ones I faced, their eyes and fangs dripping with blood. I flip to the lake of blood again, my thumb running over a stuck page I hadn't noticed before. Carefully, I peel it free.

Designs of thorns and dead flies wrap around a poem.

To the young ones who fall and do wicked deeds:
The monsters will find you and pull you like weeds.
Roaming forever until you are dead.
Hunting together until they are fed.
But only through the darkest of hours.
Some may last before fate devours.
A nightmare repeats, but this is much worse.
You can't outrun the Blacknoc Curse.

Heart pounding, I jump up. My chair crashes to the floor. The illustrations of the monsters swallowing kids swarm my mind. The story was only meant to scare children into not doing wrong. It wasn't supposed to be real.

I grip my head, rocking back and forth. This can't be happening.

To the young ones who fall and do wicked deeds.

My stomach twists and threatens to propel my meal up my throat. That man at the market. His face stretched in pain. But it wasn't my fault. I don't deserve this.

I don't!

The monsters will find you and pull you like weeds.

"No," I shout, shoving the book to the floor. It lands open to a paragraph barely visible enough to read. In crimson ink, it bleeds out the words.

You can't outrun the Blacknoc Curse.

You can't outrun the Blacknoc Curse.

You can't outrun the Blacknoc Curse.

"Are you okay?" The librarian frowns. He stands in the doorway and then points at my picnic basket on the table. "Hey! No food a—" Mr. Alden's gaze moves to the book on the floor. "The Blacknoc book? You found it?"

There's no time to explain. Over his shoulder in a small stained-glass window of a river, the sun quickly descends. *No.*

No. I can't go back!

Grabbing the book and slamming it shut, I dash out of the room and find the spiral stairs leading to the basement, where I lock myself in with a chair propped against the door. If I'm trapped here, the Blacknoc Curse can't get me.

The book burns in my grasp. I hiss, tossing it on the ground.

It falls open to the bleeding page again.

You can't outrun the Blacknoc Curse.

You can't outrun the Blacknoc Curse.

You can't outrun the Blacknoc Curse.

"No!"

I kick the tome against a wall, grab a hanging torch, and light the book on fire. Flames lick the cover and edges of the pages.

The walls rattle, the same vibrations as the first night the curse took me.

I slump to the ground and hug my knees. I can't go back. No, not to face those creatures again. Their pounding paws drum my chest. The snarls and teeth sink into my heart. I can't go back. I can't.

The second I blink, it's as if massive talons toss me onto the dirt floor. I'm back in the dark forest.

I gape at how powerful this dark magic must be to transport me so fast into this misery. The power of the Blacknoc witch. The illustrations of her madness flash across my mind, and I tense. What happened to her was horrible, but she had no right to do this to me, or to

Samuel, or anybody else. My hands ball into fists.

Pushing to my feet, I listen. The monsters are out there, breaking and snapping everything in their path. They're coming for me.

My heavy breathing quickens. I remember what Samuel said about them being sensitive to sound. As best I can, I focus on slow breaths through my nose and trudge forward. Something small dashes onto my path. I freeze. A rabbit with a swollen, raw hump on its back, stands on its hind legs, showing off fangs protruding from under its twitching nose. A shriek forms at the back of my throat, but I swallow it down. After getting a good look at me, the rabbit scurries off into the brush. I let out a breath of relief. What is wrong with this place? Despite how hideous that rabbit appeared, Samuel still took the ugly show by far.

I stifle a grunt. And yet I find myself wanting to see Samuel's face once more. I pray he finds me before the other beasts do.

I pause. Am I ridiculous to hope one monster will find me over the others?

That he will try to save me?

Chapter Four

A two-headed deer with black hide and wrinkly snout crosses my path. It pauses and stares at me. In one leap, it bounds out of sight into the brush.

The forest animals here look as ugly as the next, as if they mirror the face of the curse. Crows with pimpled beaks and pointy teeth. Moose with tumors and an intimidating mane stretching past their antlers. At least the creatures are harmless, to us monsters at least. I suspect the witch who created the curse made the mutant animals to further push the kids into fear, making it easier for monsters to find them. Good thing a two-headed beast didn't scare me.

The only thing worth resting eyes on out here is a girl like Layla. I recall the way the sunrays graced her delicate face. Am I selfish to want to see her again? I shouldn't desire her. Not here, in this horrible realm.

But something on Layla's face last night made me think of a future outside this looped prison. What it would be like to return home? To hear Pa's voice and eat his famous pies?

I should not entertain such thoughts, but I can't deny what Layla made me feel. Hope. If I had any sense left, I'd know better than to take pleasure in such delusions. There is no hope. Fate knows I'm getting what I deserve. Monsters like me don't get second chances.

It doesn't take me long to find Layla's trail. Then it goes cold, and I struggle to find her autumn scent. Relying on the imprints of her feet, I follow them to a lake tucked in the forest and surrounded by brush and weeds. But where is she?

There! I spot her on the lake. My heart sinks. She floats on her back. Filth covers her head to toe, as if something dragged her through the mud.

She's dead.

I rush to the shore. The thick claws protruding from my toes dip into the water. As if sensing me, Layla looks up and meets my gaze. Recognition fills her eyes. Does she actually distinguish me over the others?

She gives a faint smile. She doesn't seem hurt. Just cautious. I push into the water, my huge mass creating ripples that race to her. I'm not a bad swimmer. I used to swim in the streams all the time when I was human.

As I make my way toward Layla, she leans back in hesitation. Then she swims closer, her lips parting.

"What are you doing?" I say.

She straightens, her feet kicking below her, and her arms circling beside to keep her afloat. Her hand reaches out and sails over the ripples spreading around her. "I thought the algae and mud would help mask my scent."

My grin spreads. Smart girl. Not like the other kids full of despair. It explains why her trail suddenly ended. Green slime and mud cover her exposed skin. She looks horrible, but the muddy texture slowly sliding off her skin somewhat resembles my face. Thick clumps slip off her cheeks. I fight a chuckle.

"I'm impressed. How do you know this? And that

spear from the other night?"

Layla's head tilts as she leans to float on her back again. "Grandfather is a hunter. He taught me a few things. But nothing as glamorous as what you can do."

I can't help but draw closer to her. "What do you mean?"

"The trick you did with the plants. It was like nothing I've ever seen. Magic? How was any of that possible? The other monsters don't do magic, nor do they talk. Are you a witch?"

I shrug. "No, not that I'm aware of. I gained these powers recently. Only had them for a month I guess, all starting the day I was given free will to resist my monster compulsions. But last night was different." My fur quivers. "If you can believe it, under this flesh, I'm just an eighteen-year-old boy. Well, I was. Hard to imagine it's been three years." I pause and swallow hard. Has it really been that long?

She tilts her head to the side, her eyes sparkling under the moonlight. Her warm breath is refreshing. Like life. Not the evil that surrounds me daily.

"Can't you just use your powers to kill those monsters and get us out of here?" She points at my claws.

I shake my head. "Monsters can't die. That's part of the curse. I think the only way to kill them is to kill the curse. But who can do that when we're all trapped here?"

"But don't you see? You're like a miracle. You're already revolting against the curse. Completely defying it."

I'd contemplated her observations long ago. My wonderings hadn't provided answers. "Not really. It doesn't change what I am. Or allow me to escape this hell."

As if talking more to herself than me, she says, "But there was nothing about you in the book. No mention of a creature with powers like yours."

"What book?"

"*The Blacknoc Curse*. I went to the library today trying to find a clue. Something that could help me break this curse." She frowns. "I can't live like this. There has to be a way out of here."

I don't know who is more delusional. Me thinking I can save her from the inevitable, or her thinking she can escape.

But is Layla so wrong to believe in such a thing? Maybe I should save her from the pain I've endured. Just open my jaw wide and stretch it around her.

My chest constricts. I should eat my tongue for thinking such a thing, but I can't help it when the nature of my curse tries to resurface. It's like a faint voice not my own wanting me to return to the monster. "The Blacknoc book? You mean the story of a witch getting revenge on the two boys that killed her son? I know the story. I also know it won't help."

She slaps at the water, splashing me in the face. "How can you be so hopeless? I have to try. I won't remain stuck here."

I shake the water away from my face like a dog, spotting her enough to wash the mud from her face. "Have you forgotten why you're here to begin with?"

Her eyes widen. I almost regret the words, but she needs to understand where her actions led her. The same consequences brought me here, brought us all here. We aren't the victims, and we fail to remember that.

Her breath trembles. "I didn't mean it…"

My upper lip curls into a snarl. It's the same line I'd told myself. "It's only when we're punished for our actions that we don't mean them."

She runs a hand through her wet hair. "What are you saying? That I should just accept my fate? Well, I can't. And I refuse to be—"

"Like me."

Layla swims to shore, talking too loudly over her shoulder, as I follow. "If you believe in punishment so much, why don't you eat me?"

The girl shouldn't tempt me, especially when a surprising urge tells me to bite her. Ignoring the compulsion, I watch her pick up another spear she clearly made. She steps closer, the top of her head barely meeting my chest.

She looks up at me. "Wait a minute. What if you *did* actually eat me? Maybe I'll just end up like you with powers. You're different. Maybe you would transform me into good."

The idea isn't half bad, but it's not an option. "I can't risk that. If you end up like the rest, I'll have to fight you. You'll lose every piece of yourself, including your mind. You may not even remember me."

Layla huffs. "Then what is the plan? How am I getting out of here?"

Knots tighten in my stomach. She'll finally realize there is no way out.

"For now, I keep you and the others safe. I-I don't know what else. It's the best I can do for you."

She steps closer to me. "Why save me? What are you getting out of this?"

I haven't addressed the answer, let alone said it out loud. Instead, I blurt the first thing that comes to my mind.

"Because you're worth saving. I don't care what you did, you're still worth saving."

Surprise fills her eyes. My words are something I wish someone would have said to me as they fought to keep me from the beast that I am. I continue the rest of my truth. "Everyone is worth saving. At least that's what I chose to believe when I was given a second chance. I also believe that if I can save as many as possible, then the curse will spare everyone from becoming this." I gesture at myself.

"And have you?"

"Have I what?"

"Saved others?" She arches her brow.

"You're alive, aren't you?" I grin. "You and many others. At least it stops those Rock Brains from multiplying."

Water drips from Layla's long hair, and she shivers. A faint smile creeps across her cracked lips. "So, you're not so hopeless after all. But obviously sparing us from the jaws of the curse does nothing. It just keeps coming until it's fed. That's how the curse goes. 'Roaming forever until you are dead. Hunting together until they are fed.' "

"I know how it goes," I say more sharply than intended.

Everyone knows that stupid poem. A shiver makes my thorns flex. To change my focus, I breathe in her warm scent, thinking of life again, like the way a plant takes in the sun to sprout higher. She is a force of nature, compelling me to protect her, but I can't ignore a rising voice egging me to take her into my mouth and bite. Why does remaining around her surface my old monster urges so strongly? The others never had that effect on me. They also never made me feel the most human.

I clear my throat. "Not to frighten you, but if I ever act…differently. Feral. I want you to run away from me. Use your spear. Do whatever you can to stay safe."

Her hand stretches toward me, as if to caress my cheek. I step back before Layla can prick herself on my face. It pains me. I crave physical touch, something to make me feel comfort. But as long as I remain in this form, I'm not worth touching, or hurting such delicate hands.

Her chin rests flat on the opposite side of her spear. Her grin grows, seemly melting my thick hide.

"Considerate and gentle. You really aren't like the others."

Wings lift my chest. A gleam touches her eyes. To have someone see me differently than the hide that covers me is a dream I only imagine among the stars.

"Just a Samuel for now." I grin, imagining my fangs above my horned chin to be the most repulsive sight to endure.

"Samuel," she says for the first time and smirks. "How about—"

A monster launches from behind a tree after Layla. I barely stand in the way of its attack. Our momentum slams into Layla, sending her splashing into the lake. The monster swims after her.

"Layla!"

Roaring, I dive in and swim toward the massive beast. My claws sink into a thick leg, and I yank. The monster tries to wiggle free, but I climb up its body, using my horned elbows to anchor into its skin. A cloud of black blood surrounds us, so thick I can barely see the lambent moon hinting the directions of up and down.

Above me, Layla kicks toward shore.

A muffled scream erupts. I thrust to break the surface, and my eyes widen.

A second fuming savage towers over her with a spear stuck in its eye. It whines and growls, trying to pluck the object out.

I reach the shore before it can pounce on Layla. Shoving myself between them, I thrust my paw against the tip of the spear sticking out of the beast. I must push it farther into the foul flesh.

The monster yelps as I scan for Layla.

In the tall grass, she hides within the ribcage of a skeleton moose.

"Look out!" she screams.

I whirl too late. The monster I'd sunk in the lake slams me to the ground and claws at my face mercilessly. A slice of my cheek flies away. Another across my head gone. Blood drips down my chin. I moan. The other monster, already adapting to the pain, has given up on the spear in its eye. It races toward Layla.

Taking aim, I flick my wrist at her, aiming my powers.

Weeds crawl up around each bone of the skeleton cage until she's safely inside a thick cocoon.

Relieved she's protected, I can focus on battling the other two. My body tries to heal itself. The monster on top of me continues to claw at me. I grab its shoulders and roll the monster under me where I bite into its neck. A chunk of its flesh rips out in my jaw. It wails. I stand and tackle the other beast by Layla.

"Samuel!" Layla's screams are muffled. Her fists pound the cocoon.

The beast I tore into is already healing from its neck wound and heading my way to join its friend. I have to hold them off, just long enough for the sun to come up. Baring my teeth, I receive bites and lacerations from the two beasts.

Chapter Five

Grandfather sits across the table from me, his scowl piercing.

"I told you. I fell into a hunting trap." The beast that slammed into me last night left some nasty marks along my right side, but not nearly as bad as what Samuel endured.

"What kind of trap?"

"I don't—i-it was like a thorned pit."

"Never heard of such a thing." He runs a hand through his hair. "What aren't you telling me, Layla?"

"I was with a friend." I pause. Why would I call Samuel a friend? But he is, isn't he? A friend trapped under that hideous hide. "It wasn't his fault. I wasn't paying attention to where we were running in the forest and I fell. But he helped me." Helped me plenty. Saved my life. Again.

Grandfather frowns, and his fingertips tap beside his mug on the table. "A friend, huh? Could that be the reason why you're running off at night? I am so disappointed, Layla. You will answer for your behavior by not leaving your room for months."

"Grandfather, please—"

"What's this boy's name?" His tone is anything but reasonable.

"Samuel." I give Grandfather a pleading look. "He's very sweet. And protective." Even from himself.

His jaw sets firm as he points at my wrapped wounds. "I can see that. He's trouble, Layla. Stay away from him. Do you hear me?"

Grandfather only wants to keep me safe, but he can't. No amount of his punishment will keep me in this house or keep the curse from reaching me.

Grandfather waves his hand from across the table. "Do you understand me?"

"Yes, Grandfather."

"And I mean it. I don't want you seeing that boy again."

I nod. Even if I really want to avoid him, I can't. I will see Samuel in just a few hours, along with fangs and screaming. Chaos all around me.

Familiar words storm back. *You can't outrun the Blacknoc Curse.*

The pricks and stabs in my side are nothing compared to the torment this curse brings. And I don't know what's worse anymore: running forever or getting eaten.

I have to leave Grandfather. He thinks I'm locked in my room where he banished me, but I sneak out the window. I can't be here. Sitting around and waiting will not help. I must find answers. The moment I finish saddling my horse behind the barn where Grandfather can't see me, I ride out on the path to Grutchburg City.

****

I don't know why I think the library will help. Maybe because it's supposed to hold wise knowledge. But all the books in this building can't save me. I'm doomed to an eternal hell.

Folks pass me by as I wander aimlessly. They're going about their day, not dreading tomorrow. As I turn the corner of one of the bookshelves, a hand reaches out and grips my ear. I yelp and glance up at the librarian.

"You! Yesterday, a very precious book was set aflame in the basement. I know you were the last one to have it. I saw you go in there." He frowns, and then pauses as if unsure. "Not sure how you escaped. Must have scurried out like a rat."

"Please, Mr. Alden…" I hold onto his arm to keep the strain off my ear. "It was me. You're right." The Blacknoc Curse is already after me so there's no sense lying about it now. "But I was upset. I had to burn it."

He lets go of my ear, now intrigued. "Why?"

"Because I'm cursed. By the Blacknoc Curse."

After a short pause, he laughs, tossing his head back. As if he remembers he's in a library, he cringes and squeezes his lips into a tight line.

When I stand unblinking, he straightens. I sigh. "I don't expect you to believe me. My own grandfather doesn't believe me."

"I can see why." He rubs his clean chin. "You like telling tales, eh? Then be a writer. Not a vandal."

Why did being an adolescent make my claim any less valid? "You don't understand. I didn't mean to burn the book. It just upset me."

"Understandable. The illustrations are graphic. But that did not give you the right to burn it. Luckily, the damage you inflicted didn't consume the precious pages."

It wasn't luck. It is evil. I pause, recalling the graphic illustrations. I don't know why I hadn't considered this before. Someone must have known a great deal about the curse to have drawn those detailed pictures. Now for a leap of faith.

"Is there any way I can view the book again?" I say.

"After what you did? Never."

"Please. What if I only view it in your presence?" I stare at him desperately. "I need to take one last look at it. I have to know who wrote that book."

Mr. Alden gives a light chuckle. "It was written anonymously. No one knows who wrote it. Even if I knew, the author would be long dead by now. That book is over a hundred years old. And *you* burned it!"

"But I need to know how one breaks the curse."

He shakes his head and sighs. "The curse isn't real. It was only meant to scare children like yourself. And by the looks of it, it's doing a mighty fine job."

"Then humor me. Please just let me take one last look at it. I won't even touch it."

He huffs and then grips my arm to pull me into an empty reading room. "No thanks to you, I'm reconstructing the book. All the pages have been detached from its original spine and it needs a new one. Most of the damage was done to the cover, thankfully. I don't know why I'm bothering with you, but I will need some material to recreate the book cover. Since you're the one who ruined it, I figure helping me is the least you can do. I already have the boards, but I need hide."

I feel my own eyes spark. "My grandfather! He's a hunter. I can easily supply you with hide. Just give me the measurements and I'll get it."

The librarian grins, as if waiting for my condition. And yes, I did have one. "If I do this for you, can I look at the book?"

"You aren't doing me any favors. You're the one who ruined it to begin with, remember?"

It's better than no. I have to believe I can get on this man's good side and gain access to that book. Curse that book! And this curse. It's brought me nothing but trouble and pain. I'm not sure if I'll be able to resist setting the pages aflame again.

The long trip back home feels eternal. My horse wants to rest, but I have to push it. There is no time to waste.

The brown cottage fills my view. A blanket of ivy climbs up the wall, wraps around the two front windows, and stretches to the sloped roof. Grandfather's horse is gone. He must be searching for me. I take a glance inside through the kitchen window. The empty house confirms my speculations. On the side of the cottage, I search Grandfather's work shed for flesh already cleared of hair. In the far corner, there is a fair amount of goat skin attached to a wooden frame, taut like a flexed muscle. Grandfather will skin me himself if I take a piece of his livelihood.

I berate myself as I snatch the goat skin. Here I am again, taking something that does not belong to me. Can the curse further punish me for it? Fire boils inside me. My lungs burn to release my frustration. I shout, scaring away the squawking birds on the roof.

After collecting myself, I hurry back to the library, berating myself for taking the hide. I pray this hide will please the librarian enough to let me look at the book once more.

Pushing through the massive doors, I sprint across the lobby and nearly crash into the librarian's desk.

"Here." I toss the hide wrapped and tucked neatly in a satchel onto his desk.

Mr. Alden blinks. "Goodness, girl. Did you sprout

wings and fly back here?"

"I'm losing time. Can you fix it now?"

He squints, taking the satchel in his arms. "There's something I want to show you."

Great. More chores. I'm ready to roll my eyes but remember I need to get in his good graces. As I follow reluctantly, he takes me a level below to a small room packed with full bookshelves of books and scrolls that appear too old to read or in need of serious repair.

He gestures at a round table standing in the far corner. On the table are the two hundred and twenty-five pages of the book I ruined. They lay across in fifteen rows of fifteen.

Considering what they've been through, the pages aren't that devastated. And Mr. Alden clearly did a good job of cleaning the ash stains off them. But the handy, clean work is probably not what he wants me to see. The way the pages are laid out, each drawing of vines and trees, on the upper, center, or bottom pages creates a subtle twist of letters connecting to each other. A diagonal message I'd never seen before starts at the top left corner and ends at the bottom right.

"Eye for an eye?" I blurt.

He nods. "I've seen nothing like it. What does it mean?"

I shrug. "Why are you asking me? You're the librarian."

He frowns. "Well, I thought with your obsession over this book, you would have a clue about its meaning."

Reading it again myself, this time I let it digest despite everything that tells me not to listen to it, like my flesh screaming against it. *Eye for an eye*. It's a common phrase.

Mr. Alden interrupts me. "Eye for an eye. Could that be a password of some sort?"

I take a deep breath as the walls of the room rattle. It's time. I make sure to stand in front of the librarian so he can witness the truth.

"You're about to see something. And I don't want you to freak out too much. I need you to believe it's real." I turn and gesture at the table full of the pages. "The Blacknoc Curse is alive, and I can't escape it. Night is nearly here, and it's coming for me as I speak." My voice trembles and I can't stop my eyes from watering. I shake my head. "I'm so scared. Please help me."

And that's the last I'm able to say before I'm thrown back into the forest. It's hard to comprehend that just moments before I stood with Mr. Alden in a building full of people. Now, I'm alone. Vulnerable and weak.

I have no will to run this time, so I climb the nearest tree and wait. A strange-looking crow hops close to me and hisses, flashing sharp teeth. If that so-called bird was the first thing I saw on day one in the forest, I might have screamed. Instead, I break a stick off and swing it at the ugly bird.

"Shoo!"

It flaps out of the tree, squawks, and leaves me be. Good riddance.

I suck in air and carefully release it, trying to transport my mind to a place of peace. The stars are so entrancing up here, they could almost make me forget the evil that lurks beneath.

Unshed tears burn my eyes. Am I a hypocrite to

call the monsters evil? Samuel's words return like a hammer. *It's only when we're punished for our actions that we don't mean them.*

That day at the market. The horror on that man's face pokes holes into my chest. I caused him so much pain. And for what? I deserve this fate. It is my fault. I glance at the long way down to the forest floor, wondering if the fall will kill me.

Subtle scratching on bark startles me. I twist to view Samuel hanging below on a branch, gazing at me.

"How did you—" I start to say.

"I have claws, and I can climb." He grins as he balances on a branch to inch across from me. "Not a great place to be, Layla."

"I'm aware. I'm just so tired of running."

"I know the feeling."

I lean in. "I caused a lot of trouble at the library. Burned the Blacknoc book. Now, I have to help the librarian fix it."

His strong claws grip the branch he sits on, bending it under his weight. "So, let me get this straight. The Blacknoc Curse is after you, and you're still wreaking havoc?"

Cute. "It's not like that. I told you I was trying to find a clue in the book. I just got so mad and burned it. I regret it now. Just like everything else. I regret so many things." My voice lowers to a whisper, my elbows squeezing into my sides. "Samuel, I deserve to be here, not to be saved. You're wrong to think I'm worthy of saving. I-I am a monster." I sniffle.

"Layla, listen." His paw hovers over my knee as if to touch it but then he retreats. Any touch from his hide will hurt. He's unwilling to harm me. "We're capable of making terrible mistakes, even wicked ones." His muscular shoulders flex, making his sharp fur appear to spike. "But it's not right for this curse to judge us because of it. The only one who can judge me is the Creator."

I shake my head, whimpering. "You don't know what I did." My eyes water. "I was at Rydmont's city market when I reached into a stranger's pocket. The man screamed that he had been robbed. The officers came, and I panicked. I pointed at the old man across from me, even tossed the watch at his feet. I shouted, 'It was him. I saw him take your watch!' The man was mute and couldn't defend himself. The officers grabbed him, but they didn't take him to prison." My throat swells. "The man I'd stolen from was filthy rich and demanded he be left alone with the old man."

Tears run down my face. "The next thing I knew, the old man ran out of an alley, his hand completely gone. I can't forget the blood running down his arm. The way he cradled it. The horror in his eyes."

I shake uncontrollably now. "Oh, I'm so sorry. I'm so sorry," I try to say louder, but Samuel hushes me. "It's all my fault," I whisper.

Samuel bows his head, giving me a minute, and then his eyes meet mine. He reaches for my face but then pulls back again.

"You know there was a time when I was a monster, too."

I wipe my runny nose. "What do you mean?"

"I mean the real reason why I'm here." He pauses, glaring between the branches at the drop between us. "I killed."

His sandy eyes study mine, as if waiting for me to

reprimand him. I swallow hard. "Killed?"

He shakes his head, a tear getting lost in the fur around his eye. "Back home, I often kept to myself, until I couldn't anymore. I got involved with a group of boys. They made me feel important, like a part of a brotherhood. But to stay in Rogue Remains—what they called themselves—I had to go through an initiation.

I followed them into the woods, holding tight to the end of a leash. Tied to a stray dog we'd found. Nobody saw us that day, only the boys who kept shouting at me to do it. I thought if I could prove to them I was tough enough to kill an animal, that it would be the key to letting me become one of them…" He raises his hand, as if holding an invisible object, and instantly slams it down into his lap. "But instead I became something worse. And not a day goes by that I don't regret it."

He belts out a roar that finishes with a howl. I turn my head and grip a branch for support. Thrumming rattles my chest. I can't judge him. I did a bad thing, too. I force myself to scoot closer to him, leaning enough to smell the dirt and foliage stuck to his fur like stickers. For a split second, I see a hideous monster again.

"And then the curse took you?"

Samuel nods. "I remember little. Just preparing to go to bed and, in an instant, I was in a forest I'd never seen before, and I know all the forests near my home. I spent the next five nights running until…I gave up. I decided I deserved to get eaten. And transformed into this." He glances at his limbs as if they're rotten.

"How many?"

"How many what?"

I swallow. Daring to ask. "How many have you

eaten?"

Shame seems to weigh his head down. "Too many to count, but not as many as I've saved in the short time I've been able to."

"How long have you been saving others?"

His ears twitch back. "About a month."

"But how were you able to stop eating them? The legend of the curse is that *all* monsters eat the wicked children."

"For three years, I fed." He winces, as if something slapped his face. "You don't know what it was like, constantly driven to torment and not having control of your own actions. I felt every wicked deed they'd ever done. I can still taste the wickedness of each kid as they slid down my throat, and I wanted more."

"No, I don't suppose I could ever imagine." A part of me is repulsed as I envision him clawing and chewing me up as he did the others. But who am I to judge? I'd caused much pain to an innocent.

He continues. "The first night I stopped feeding, I was chasing a boy. At least I thought I was, but this boy moved impossibly fast. When I finally cornered him, my eyes deceived me. It…it was the dog, the same chocolate-colored dog I'd killed." His hands shake, and it's the first visible sign of fear I've seen from him. "The dog was larger than I remember. It sat in front of me unafraid, almost as if it wanted to play. And I remember this terrible pain in my chest. I couldn't hold it in. For the first time, I felt something other than my monster urges. I wept, drowning in sorrow. I must have apologized to the dog a hundred times, begging for it to forgive me…It walked up to me and licked my toe. And then it was gone." He shrugs. "I don't know what it did to me, but I haven't eaten a kid since."

My amazement takes over. How is that even possible? "Do you think the dog was real? I mean, have you seen it since?"

"I haven't. It was like a ghost. There one minute and then gone the next. All I know is something changed me that day. And I figured using my new abilities to protect kids was my version of gratitude."

I frown. "But monsters are slaves to the Blacknoc Curse, forever tormented by a lustful drive to eat evil children. What happened to you is impossible. Could it have been you were chosen for a reason? Maybe your heart could not live with what you did and that somehow counteracted the curse? Monsters are not supposed to feel sorry or remorse."

He grins, showing his fangs. I refrain from wincing. "That's a nice theory to wrap up my awful past into a pretty bow, but I doubt it. As far as I'm concerned, I'm still getting what I had coming, but at least this time I can change the outcome for others."

"Help me!" a boy cries in the distance.

I eye Samuel, appreciating his sandy eyes barely visible under his fur. I can't decide what he is. He's a monster and yet he's not. "Go save him. Please. He probably needs saving more than I do."

"No, Layla. I believe no matter how awful we are, we all deserve another chance." He winks. "Stay safe. I'll be back."

Samuel lowers himself, using each branch to break his fall with his powerful feet, and lands on the ground with a thud. In seconds, he's out of sight.

A hair-raising roar flings my attention in the opposite direction. Following shortly is another scream.

This one is a young girl. I must be out of my mind because I quickly climb down the tree, though not as gracefully as Samuel. I land smack on my back.

Moaning, I scramble up and dart for the distress call. Following the girl's loud footsteps and a trail of broken twigs, I catch up to her and tackle her to the ground. My hand smothers her mouth.

I don't know what's come over me.

She struggles under my grip. Blonde hair sticks to her wet rosy cheeks. She's half my size. She can't be any older than eleven. What could an eleven-year-old have possibly done?

"You need to be quiet," I hiss. "These things are sensitive to noise."

She nods and I let her up. "Who—"

"Layla."

"Molly." Her head tilts up at me as she rubs the back of her neck.

"Molly, stay close. And don't make a sound."

I will not run. *We* will not run. I must look as if I'm losing my mind as I search for a good stick, because Molly is not keeping close. She forms distance between us.

"What are you doing?" she whispers.

I hush her and then find what I'm looking for, bone dry wood and a sturdy stick. I pluck dry grass and rest it on my piece of wood. I cut a notch into the wood with a rock and shove bark under the notch.

"Hold the wood down," I urge Molly. "Don't let it slip."

She nods and places her small hands on the wood, her fingers shaking.

"Still please," I warn.

I rest my spindle on the groove and begin spinning it between my hands as fast as I can.

Grandfather made sure I could make one of these on my own. After a hundred failed attempts, he said we weren't going home until I could cook the quail we'd killed. Blisters had marked my palms for days. But I now know what it takes to keep going until a spark flares beneath my fingers.

A glowing ember ignites. I tap the fire board to allow my ember to settle onto the piece of bark. Carefully, I transfer the bark to my ball of tinder. I quickly blow against it, careful not to blow too hard.

A stream of fire rushes up, and I grin.

If this curse treats me like a monster, then I'll act like one.

Chapter Six

After grabbing and tossing the monster down a bank, I encourage the little boy to run with me.

He's pale and quivering, but he stays behind me.

I have to find Layla. When I left her, I'd seen something all too familiar. That despair in her eyes. I knew that look all too well. I should've never mentioned my encounter with the ghost dog. Maybe she figures out that there is no end. That even someone like me who refuses the curse is not exempt from its hold.

I swear at the sky. I want to tell Layla I'm sorry. Sorry I can't rescue her like she wants. Sorry I can't free every child from the curse, especially the little boy following me.

The boy sniffles and mumbles, "It found me. The curse. It's punishing me for horrible things I did to my teacher." His weeping explodes.

I often see the same pattern among the ones I save. They admit to their wicked deeds after I've rescued them. As if my act of choosing to save them instantly causes them unbearable guilt. They have no choice but to confess their sins as if I'm a priest.

I fight a grin. As if.

"Listen, kid, we're all here for the same reason. But no amount of guilt will change anything."

It never mattered how many times I said sorry. It changed nothing.

"But how did the curse find *me*?" the boy whines. "No one knew what I did. I'm a chronic liar, and that never got me into trouble before. So why now? Surely, others have done far worse than me."

The curse is a mystery to everyone, but I have my speculations.

I shake my head. "I don't know, kid. My guess is, whatever the sin, it's the one that screams the loudest. Maybe the choice we make comes from a place inside us that's darker than our nightmares, something we never thought we'd ever do, and that gets the curse's attention." I groan, not wanting to ask him to tell me his wicked deed. He doesn't have to tell me. None of them do. And I've heard so many deeds, I can't stomach another.

The boy gasps.

I rotate to find the source of his reaction. In between the trees, a sliver of fire twirls in the night air. On the other end of the flames, a monster yelps, clawing at its face. It's on fire.

"Come on." An invisible fist clutches my heart.

The boy hesitates to follow me toward the chaos ahead. My speed picks up the moment I see who wields the torch.

Layla.

Something in my stomach drops. I feel as if I've swallowed a drug making everything around me bigger. My vision blurs, but I ignore it.

Undergrowth burns in a circle around her and another girl. Outside that circle are four pacing monsters. My pulse quickens.

Layla thrusts the torch out, threatening to step close to the flaming circle just to burn the monster again. The monster with its face on fire hisses at the walls of flames between it and its prey.

I reach the flaming circle. “Layla!”

Ignoring me, she raises her flame, fury burning in her eyes. She growls back at the beasts as the girl clings behind her. A beauty so angry, I fear for her sanity. For a split second, I imagine Layla as a monster. I won’t allow her to become that.

One beast dares to cross the fire. Shards of flames catch the edges of its dry fur, which quickly spread across its whole body. The monster wails but continues to press forward.

Before it can reach the girls, I run on all fours, finding it more difficult than usual on my paws, and race through the flames. My hide catches fire. I groan as I tackle the monster.

We’re both on fire, carving each other up. Black blood spots the ground. The stench of burnt flesh reaches me. Roaring in each other’s faces, I punch the monster in the jaw and kick it back into the fire where it wails and darts away to put out its own anguish.

My fist absorbs the pain. It takes longer to self-heal my blistered hide. Flames continue to stick to the edges of my sharp coat like bugs, crawling along my body. I roar, thrashing myself on the cool dirt.

The girl shielded by Layla screams as another monster leaps on top of me. Then another pins me down. They’re stronger than I remember. Or I’m weaker.

Layla launches the torch at their backs. They turn their attention to her, letting me stand. I groan as Layla picks up another torch by her boots and thrusts it in front of her to singe the nearest snout. She dives and rolls back to avoid an incoming swing. I can't believe my eyes or the courage she uses to fight these hideous creatures three times her size.

The boy I'd saved earlier is nowhere to be found. There's no time to search for him. A fourth monster slips past Layla and tackles the little blonde girl. With no time to worry about my wounded and burnt body, I go after the beast extending its jaw over the blonde girl.

The second I leap in midair, the monster turns and smacks me with its paw to the ground. I scramble up and stretch my fingers toward the flames. Not knowing what to expect, I expel all the power I have left. As I concentrate, the flames turn blue and rise higher and twist, bending like spikes at each snarling jaw. The flaming circle inverts, trapping the monsters.

They roar and swat at the flames.

Layla rushes toward me. Her eyes widen, as though she doesn't recognize me.

"Samuel?"

I glance at my body. My frame is slightly smaller. The dense needle-like fur shrinks to thinner hairs, and the underfur of tiny barbs are nearly gone.

Impossible. I'm changing. The horns on my elbows, chin, and skull scale down to dull points. The weapons of torment are tamed. In a sense, I must appear like a deformed beast.

Layla points at the sky. The sun is rising. The rays find the top of my head where it burns worse than the fire could ever hurt me.

I hiss as I scramble back into the shadows. My power over the monsters disintegrates. The sun forces them to scurry off into the unknown. I'm left to take one last glance at Layla.

She smiles, and rushes into the shadows with me, her hands reaching up to cup my cheeks. My thin fur still scratches her. She winces, but her smile stays strong. Reassurance sweeps over me, warming my heart.

Before I go into my grave, Layla pulls me closer.

"I'm going to get us out of here."

****

After I storm into the library, I find Mr. Alden in our regular private room. Mr. Alden lifts his gaze away from the Blacknoc book on the table. He stares at me as if he's seen a ghost. His lower lip parts. I can tell it's not disbelief he struggles to grasp. It's belief. That's all I can ask for. I just want someone to believe me. I let him take in my presence a bit longer before taking a seat across from him.

"I can't believe I'm saying this, but…" He rakes a hand through his hair. "The message in the pages. You vanishing right before my eyes." He slowly stands and then paces. "I-I think I believe you. I saw it in your eyes that night. You can't fake that. True fear." He folds an elbow on top of his arm and grips his chin. "You are truly cursed, aren't you?"

I nod. "And I'm trying to break it. That's why I needed to further study that book."

"Of course." His fingers grip the edges of the table. "This might actually make sense. The kids that go missing each year without a trace. It's the curse's doing, isn't it?"

"Most likely, yes. And there's no telling how many are cursed or how many are transformed. I'm lucky to make it out alive each night."

I see the wheels turning in his head.

“But how are you not a monster by now?” he says.

After telling him to take a seat, I explain everything. Samuel, the other monsters, and Samuel’s powers. He appears particularly fascinated with Samuel.

“Magnificent. But how is that possible?”

“I’ve wondered the same thing. He’s a miracle, a rebel against the curse.”

Hope rises in his face. He picks up the Blacknoc book, the pages loose in its cover.

“Careful with that,” I warn.

“Why?”

“There’s something not right with that book. The day I burned it, the pages were bleeding.”

Mr. Alden frowns as he hesitantly skims through the pages. “There’s no blood here, girl.”

I curse, snatching for the book to see for myself. Nothing but white pages and black ink. “Well, maybe because the curse isn’t after you. It’s taunting me!” I slam the book on the table.

“Calm yourself.” He holds up his hand. “Just take a deep breath. No young girl should have to deal with this alone. I will do everything within my power to help you, okay? Let me handle the book while you calm down. We don’t want another fire incident, do we?”

Tempting. Fire is something I now welcome, and if there’s one thing I’ve learned, it is fire is an ally. I plop on a chair, caging my face with clammy fingers. My pulse slows. I’m grateful to have someone believe me, even if it is an acquaintance.

He motions beside me. “There’s nothing here about the powers you mentioned Samuel has.”

“Exactly.” I shoot up and pace.

"Maybe he's the key to breaking the curse?"

"I don't think it's that simple. He's trapped deeper than I am. He can't go home every morning like I can."

"Yes, so he's the reason for your return. What a small gift he's granted you with, but a gift nonetheless."

Fluttering stirs my insides. True, and I am grateful for him. I meant the last words I said to him. I will get him out of that hell. As long as I can still come back here to the real world every day, I will fight.

I cross my arms as I study the hidden message. *Eye for an eye.* "We still have this to decipher."

Mr. Alden's chin drops. "Retaliation, Layla, does not end well."

I shake my head. Of course, I already knew what it meant but didn't want to believe it.

He continues. "Layla, if you don't mind me asking, what did you do to get cursed?"

Chapter Seven

I cannot bring myself to admit to Mr. Alden what I'd done. I'm surprised I told Samuel, but then he had every right to know who he was protecting. No judgment came from him. That's mercy, I don't deserve. Samuel should have crucified me, should have told me I was the true monster hiding in sheep's clothing.

A long awkward pause hangs between the librarian and me as we share acquacotta soup, studying the Blacknoc book for more clues. We scatter the pages across a board nailed to the wall, rearranging them every which way to find something new, but to no avail. I already know the answer is right in front of me but don't want to accept it.

Exhaustion pummels me. I tell Mr. Alden I need a nap and to wake me in an hour. I can't afford to waste the day I have left to much-needed sleep.

Midday arrives. I'm off to deal with what's left at home. Mr. Alden thinks I'm coming back, but I'm not. He's kind to think I would feel better and shouldn't be by myself when the curse takes me. But right now, I need to address the wicked deed that cursed me.

When I return home, Grandfather whips me for sneaking off and disobeying him. More days of isolation are added to my punishment. Nails now secure my bedroom window.

As I pace, the wooden floors creak under my weight. I can't remain locked up here, no more than what I already am. I have to face my deed.

Pulling the hood of my robe over my head, I take a deep breath. Grandfather will throw away the key after this.

I burst out my room, dash across the kitchen to the entrance, and toss open the door. Grandfather scrambles from the chair to catch up, but I'm already outside, making my way to my horse.

No time for a saddle. I mount him bareback, grip his mane, and dash off.

"Layla!"

"I'm sorry, Grandfather," I shout over my shoulder. "But Samuel is in trouble."

Picking up the pace to Rydmont City, my horse flies along the narrow trail. What will Grandfather do next when I return? Cast me out and disown me?

The sun creeping down behind the treetops used to be a pleasant sight. But now it's a constant aggravator to the anxiety pounding in my chest, matching the horse's gallop.

The familiar stacks of Rydmont City greet me. Shophouses and three-level homes with high-peaked roofs and casement windows stretch across the cobblestone foundation. Stone bridges arch over the wide river, often filled with dinghies, which flows through the city. Rydmont would be lovely if the memory of my evil actions didn't lurk here. A place I tried to forget and told myself I would never return.

I dismount and start my search. People clutter the streets. It grows difficult to locate the man. Most people avoid the poor areas. I make a turn into a homeless area. Many dressed in rags can easily pass as the old man. The only problem is they all clearly have two intact hands. I leave the area and try another street when I spot a man with only a left hand. From behind a cart, I study the old man hobbling down the street. His stump brings nausea to my stomach.

I follow him.

Shoulders bump into mine, but I'm persistent and careful not to raise his suspicion. Who knows what he will do when he sees me? I deserve more than a slap to the face.

The old man takes a left in an alley behind a cathedral. With hushed steps, I inch closer.

Boards shelter a cubbyhole of the building to make a room. The old man pulls back a wooden door and slips inside his hovel.

Before he can close the door, I push it back. "I'm so sorry to intrude, but please let me explain."

He tries to close the door with his hand and stub, but my young arms easily overpower his brittle limbs. I step inside. A tiny candle glints in the corner on a wooden crate. The flame casts shadows on his horror-filled face as he recognizes me.

Heat flushes my cheeks. I shouldn't be here, causing him more pain.

The old man opens his mouth, but no sound comes out. Lips move, but nothing.

"Please. I want to apologize. I can't ever express how sorry I am, and that what happened to you should have happened to me. I was the thief. Not you. You didn't deserve it. I did."

His worried eyes settle into an emotionless expression. He has every right to not accept my apology.

"I'm truly sorry," I say again, as if repeating it will somehow make it better.

Am I really sorry? Or just saving my hide? If the curse wasn't after me, I can't say I would have apologized.

He straightens and pushes me back with his one good hand. I let him. With surprising force, he shoves me outside and slams the door in my face.

"I'm sorry," I whisper to the rickety door.

The sun winks its final goodbye. The alleyway and ground seem to shake. Nausea attacks my stomach as the curse takes me away and throws me into the forest. I was stupid to think an apology would somehow fix everything. The Blacknoc message was very clear.

I stare at my right hand.

Chapter Eight

Like no other beauty, Layla stands across from me. This time she finds me. Her dark, earthlike eyes are wide, glistening, as if she's been crying.

I rush toward her, resisting the urge to scoop her into my arms. I'll still hurt her, after all.

"What's wrong, Layla?"

Her gaze runs over the entire length of my body. Her hand stretches to hover mere inches over my shoulder and then it slowly glides down to my hand.

"Why do you look different?" Her voice is soft.

"I don't know. A lot feels different. For one, I don't heal as fast."

"You're shorter. Less muscular. Thinner fur. And your face…" Her hand reaches to my cheek, but I pull away. "Maybe I was right about you being chosen for a reason. To help me follow this decision."

She turns, but I shift with her to force her gaze on me. "What do you mean?"

Layla tells me about the Blacknoc book, and the message.

"And I need you to do me this favor," she demands. She raises her right hand and places it so delicately in front of my mouth. I stare at it like it's a foreign object. "I need you to take it. 'Eye for an eye.' "

"Are you insane? You don't even know if that's the answer."

I circle her, a predatory instinct. I force myself to stop. The idea has me flexing the thin claws I have left. She's gone mad. Nowhere does it guarantee this will work.

"Please, Samuel. I feel it in my gut that this is the right thing to do."

"What? Hurting yourself? I won't do that." Especially not when my old urges may not want just her hand.

"It's my decision." She raises her chin. "I'm not just doing this for me. I want to free you, too. Free them all."

I grit my teeth and ball my shaky paws. "I can't hurt you, Layla."

"Please. I don't have the strength to do it myself. It has to be you. I know you'll make it a clean cut."

I step back to lean against a tree for support. Eating her hand makes me sick in every way. *But eating her whole simplified things.* I pivot, cursing. What is this voice I keep hearing in my head? It's not mine and sounds almost feminine this time. I would have thought my sudden appearance change would have gotten rid of the terrible voice.

Layla inches closer, not giving me room to move, and slowly gets on her knees. Her right hand extends. She turns her gaze away, glancing over her shoulder.

I belt out a thunderous roar, startling her and the birds fluttering away from the treetops. Monsters will surely make their way here now, but I don't care. I kneel and inhale her scent, hear her tepid, shaky breath. Then grip her arm. She yelps in my grasp but keeps her head turned away.

A tear snakes down the side of her face. If ever I

needed my monster impulses, it's now because I don't have the strength to do this.

My blood heats as I extend my jaw and clamp it hard around her tiny hand. A piece of her I've wanted to hold since I met her easily slips down my throat, turning into ash in the pit of my stomach.

I let go before the voice returns. Layla lets out a blood curdling scream and collapses on her side, holding her stub.

My chests aches. I want to die.

"I'm so sorry, Layla."

She thrashes and rolls to her other side. To my surprise, her stub is not bloody. Not even bone shows. Just skin, and the resemblance of an ash stain.

All the noise has attracted several monsters, hiding behind the trees just watching. They must think I'm finally doing my job and eating wicked children. They can all go to hell.

Layla's watery gaze meets mine. "Thank you, Samuel."

In a cloud of white mist, her body shimmers away, as if on a gentle carpet, then vanishes completely.

I crash on my palms and grip the ground she'd rested on.

"Layla?"

It worked? Impossible. It actually broke the curse, but only her curse. I still remain. She's gone. And I'll never see her again.

The pack of monsters explodes in deafening roars I'd never heard before. In unity, they charge me, their heavy and powerful paws pounding the foliage.

Layla. She's gone.

In place of fear, heaviness caves into my heart.

They reach me. I don't run. Their fangs and claws sink into me.

Fool, the voice returns in a tantrum. *You let her go!*

As multiple jaws stab into me, I realize who the voice belongs to—The Blacknoc witch.

****

I'm back in Rydmont City where I'd left the old man. I sprint like a mad woman looking for my horse. The moon is full, and many folks have long gone to their dwellings. More importantly, the night sky remains, and I'm no longer cursed. It worked. But where is Samuel? And the others?

A fist squeezes my heart. If what I did only worked for me, then Samuel is still trapped.

No.

I need to find Mr. Alden.

As soon as I locate my horse, I realize how difficult not only will it be to ride a horse but doing anything else with only one hand. I gaze at my right stub. A clean cut. The wound never bled. It just closed up with a smoky finish along the stub. Maybe Samuel's powers?

The grisly sight raises bile in my throat. I don't know if I will ever get used to the stub for a hand. What will Grandfather think?

I force the thoughts aside and mount my horse. As best I can, I grip his mane with my good hand and tuck my stub under my wrist. I nearly fall off thrice once we ride. My body awkwardly moves in rhythm with my horse as my hand struggles to steady me. My thighs throb from squeezing too tight.

In a slow gait, we reach Grutchburg.

Heart beating and sweat slicking my hair back, I

hurry up the library stairs, praying Mr. Alden is still inside. He often stays late, on the hunt for clues in that stupid Blacknoc book. I bang on the tall doors until my arm grows heavy.

No one answers.

As I turn away, Mr. Alden pulls open the doors, his amber eyes restless.

"Layla? How is—" He gasps. "Good heavens. Let me see that."

I scurry in so he can study my wound. Puzzlement and horror fill his eyes. I let him take in the sight a little longer before explaining it to him.

He frowns. "You said Samuel did this to you?"

"Yes, but I asked him to. Like the message said 'eye for an eye.' "

Mr. Alden leans back in a lounge chair that's usually occupied. The regulars have long since emptied the building.

"I thought it would break the Blacknoc Curse, but it only broke mine." I slam my right stub down on the round table between us. "We must figure out a way to free him!"

The librarian rubs his eyes and then stands. "You need to rest. I desperately need rest. Go home and we will talk in the morning. Enjoy your freedom for the time being."

How can I enjoy my freedom when one of the most beautiful human beings I've ever known is suffering right now?

****

I must fight back and stay alive. If I get eaten again, something tells me I won't come back. Or at least, I won't come back with the intent to protect. I was given a second chance and can't waste it now just because Layla is gone. I can't give up.

Razor-sharp teeth gnaw at my limbs. I roar, trying to scramble to my feet, to smack the snarling snouts away from me. But I'm overpowered by the group of monsters holding me down, tearing me up.

A girl I'd seen before with Layla comes out of nowhere with two torches and launches one at a monster's back. The beast spins, scattering sparks among its friends. They bellow their misery. A boy I saved last night follows the girl with torches of his own. He lights the ground on fire in a ring. He and the girl stand inside, and they swing their fire at the beasts as if wielding swords.

The distraction allows me room to pick myself up, but I'm badly wounded. Gashes cover me, snout to paws.

The kids are still no match for the cluster of teeth surrounding them.

"Run! Get out of here!" I growl.

My legs wobble. Instead of black blood that usually oozes from my hide, it's dark red.

I must protect those kids. I may be smaller, weaker, but I still have claws and teeth.

Groaning, I leap in the air and sink my claws into the nearest beast.

Chapter Nine

The moment I push pass the fence gate and enter my cottage, the familiar solidness of the wood floor warms me. Neatly placed rocking chairs across the hearth in the parlor are welcoming. As Grandfather would have it, the kitchen is clear of spots and dust. Somehow, the roof over my head is bigger than I remember. Relief floods me. I am safe. No longer would the curse rip me away from my sanctuary. That relief diminishes when I spot Grandfather in my room, slouched by the wall on the floor. Dark bags hang under his eyes.

He's not ready to see this. Tucking my stub under my robe, I walk into my room. He looks up at me. His eyes are red and swollen.

"You came back?"

"Of course. I never wanted to leave you, Grandfather. I love you too much."

His jaw slacks. "I know it must be hard without your parents, but I'm doing what I can, and it's not enough. I'm sorry I failed you."

My chest aches. I barely knew my parents. Grandfather raised me most of my life after the plague took them. And he's been the best parental figure I could ever ask for. If only I can tell him it's not his fault, it's mine. I'm driving myself and him to insanity because of my mess.

The worse part has yet to come because Grandfather hasn't seen it yet.

I reveal my stub from under my robe and bring it to the candlelight flickering on the nightstand.

"Lord! What happened to you?" He rushes to inspect.

The truth is far from his reality, but I have to try my best to be honest. He deserves my candor. "It was all my fault, Grandfather. I was at the market when I stole from someone. I tried to take their pocket watch but got caught. It's my fault. Only my own. I'm so sorry. I failed you, Grandfather."

"Layla, what have you done?"

"What you raised me not to do. I knew better but did it anyway. And suffered the consequences."

He yanks me hard closer by the candle for further inspection. "Why does it look like that? When did this happen?"

My stub is clean, the skin on top of the bone is as smooth as taut leather. Its appearance is as supernatural as the curse. My heart lifts. I am just grateful I didn't suffer too much when Samuel swallowed my hand.

"He saved me." My eyes brim with tears. "Samuel helped seal the wound. It's a miracle heal, a kind gesture I didn't deserve."

Grandfather erupts, cursing Samuel's name to the ground, and blaming himself. For a while, he struggles to look me in the eye. His rage slackens, then he wraps his arms tight around me. I tuck my head against his neck. A blanket of safety warms me.

"I'm so sorry that happened to you," he says.

He kisses the top of my head, the way he used to whenever I'd scrape my knee or cut my arm. But no number of kisses will bring back my hand like he wishes.

We talk all that night. He's convinced my acting out is part of being an adolescent. He thinks he's reached me, but he never lost me. Or maybe he did. Maybe my decision to steal, to have the Blacknoc Curse pursue me, did take me away from him. My poor choice led me to this point. No one else is to be blamed for it.

I still have to endure my punishment for breaking out of my previous punishment Grandfather gave me. I must remain locked in my room. For a hundred years, or a less exaggerated sentence when he calms down. I have to help more around the house. Do extra chores, until my palm peels from blisters according to him. Despite all the chastening, I see the love for me in Grandfather's eyes. I am safe and I am loved.

****

After enduring weeks of Grandfather's punishment without fault, I persuaded him to let me work at the library. He heard the word "work" and Mr. Alden's positive word about me and agreed to it. I must promise to only go to the library. Grandfather will follow up on my actions.

To be honest, I enjoy spending more time around him. I missed us. But I also miss Samuel.

I'd spent countless days searching for clues. Something that would hint at how to free Samuel. Weeks turned to months. Summer came, and Grandfather's punishment lifted.

I grew desperate.

Mr. Alden warned me not to go public with what we knew that it could put him and me in the asylum. But I didn't care. I was already crazy with helplessness.

I made posters about the curse and pinned them across both cities of Grutchburg and Rydmont, hoping someone would know something and come forward. More weeks of rain washed the posters to the weeds. And then the thing I feared the most overtook me. Despair.

I gave up.

****

With the curse not seeking me anymore, I may remain in my bed. I can dream again, but the dreams are anything but welcome escapes, and often make me feel as if I'm still cursed.

Grandfather doesn't understand why I wake up screaming in the middle of the night. Monsters, I tell him. Things I fear I can't fight this time.

In this memory of a dream, Samuel stands before me. Heavy fog distorts the forest trees surrounding us. The kids he saved are shielded behind him. I'm excited to see him but when I run to him, he explodes into ash. In a slow wave, every child erupts into the same debris, floating down like snow. The ash covers me. When I raise my hand and stub to clear my vision, I can only view a thick carpet of black.

Similar nightmares continue to torment me. There isn't a day where I wake with a dry pillow.

Grandfather pokes his head into my room. "You've been stuck in this room for days. You're not punished anymore, you know. Why don't you go out?"

I don't answer but continue to gaze out the window, wondering where Samuel is. What's become of him now? A part of me hopes he's still saving lives. I wouldn't have escaped if it wasn't for him. But who will save him? It was like he said, "No matter how awful we are we all deserve another chance." He gave me mine. I'm free because of him. Yet, freedom doesn't feel like freedom at all.

Grandfather's shuffling feet startle me as he crosses the threshold to lean beside the window. He gazes out with me, his arms crossing.

"You're thinking of that boy, aren't you? What was his name again?"

A heavy boulder grows in my throat, making it difficult to swallow.

"Samuel," I whisper.

Even the taste of his name on my lips makes him more real, as if I'll see him again.

Grandfather shakes his head. "I realize I'm hard on you, but it's because I want you to be safe. I know I never gave this Samuel boy a chance, or thanked him for…" He points at my stub. "But I'll tell you what. If you bring him over for dinner sometime, maybe if I get to know him, we can see about letting you spend time with him again. What do you say, Layla?"

I turn my head to meet his sweet eyes. Torn between smiling and crying. The statement coming from Grandfather means a lot. It's as close to a blessing as I'll ever get from him. And I know he would love Samuel. But I also know it's impossible for Samuel to meet him.

A tear trails down my right cheek. I quickly turn back to the window to hide it.

"Of course," I force myself to say. "I would love for you to meet him."

I stand and hug Grandfather. Giving into the delusion that Samuel will walk through the front door of my house and sit across from Grandfather and me.

Like we're all one happy family.

A knock sounds at the door.

When Grandfather answers it, Mr. Alden stands on the doorstep. Sweat glistens along his temples. His hands are pulled tight behind him. There's an ink stain on the collar of his robe. Mr. Alden clears his throat.

"William, what brings you by? Would you like to stay for supper?"

The librarian extends a hand. "No, sir, I'm actually here for your daughter."

Grandfather shakes his hand.

"Mr. Alden?" I squeeze in. "What are you doing here?"

He clears his throat. "I still need your *help* down at the library." Then he turns back to Grandfather. "I know she quit working at the Grutchburg library, but things are no longer the same there. Havoc everywhere. Your granddaughter has been keeping it in top form. Much work is still needed…" He meets my gaze. "And I could very much use your help right now."

Grandfather pulls me into a sideways hug and grins. "Well, that's up to her. Just don't steal her away from me too long."

The librarian smiles. "I would never dream of it, sir."

I glance up at Grandfather. "May I have a moment, please?"

He pats my hair. "Of course. I'll be in the garden." He slips past Mr. Alden and walks out of sight.

"What are you doing here?" I blurt.

"I found something that might help us save Samuel." He grins.

My eyes widen. "That's impossible."

"See for yourself."

****

In our usual private room full of ruined books, I seat myself at the table that has seen a plethora of repaired books. But nothing like this Blacknoc book.

Mr. Alden is sweating, seemingly ready to trip over his own feet. He slaps the Blacknoc book's new leather cover, the title spelled in red thread. I can only assume Mr. Alden sewed the title himself.

"I'll admit I'd given up on him, too." His gaze lowers and then rises to meet mine. "Figured it was too late for the others. I'd stopped searching, and finally decided to repair the Blacknoc book. Move on as if none of it ever happened. Just stick it back on the shelf, forget it all." He wipes at his head. "But when I removed the burnt cover, an indentation was left behind on the thin wood behind it. And that's when I realized the book must have been recovered once before."

"Indentation of what?" My pulse thrums.

He rushes to a writing desk in the far corner and pulls a sheet hidden between the pages of a book. "Meet the author of the Blacknoc book."

Held in front of him is the tracing of a name smeared in coal.

Velma Blacknoc.

****

Pulling into busy Rydmont City on our horses, Mr. Alden and I decide to split up. As much discomfort as this city brings me, I shove that aside. I'm here for Samuel.

Velma Blacknoc. Someone has to know who that is. It's my only hope.

I tie the reins of my horse to a post near a shop and

start from there. Most folks don't like questions about other people, especially when it comes from adolescents. But I'm determined. I won't stop until I see a shred of familiarity the moment I utter the name to a stranger.

The sun beats down on me. The clustered street makes it hard to think. Hard to breathe. Doubt tells me I'm in over my head. That nothing I can do will save him.

Panic fills me when I spot the old man with a missing right hand strolling down the street of Arakken toward me. This is why I avoided this city. It's as if I can always feel the magnitude of my wicked deed here. But I realize this didn't just happened to me. I brought it on myself.

I swallow hard and take shelter in a tent where a vendor sells lemons and watermelons. What am I doing? There's no sense in hiding anymore. The shame and guilt will always plague me, but I have to face it.

Untucking myself from the tent, I place myself directly on his path. The old man recognizes me right away and pauses for a split second, glancing at my missing hand. His stoic face remains the same. In return, he simply nods at me and brushes past.

It's not exactly words of mercy, but there is something, if ever so little, lifted off my chest. I exhale, spinning on my heels to take in the city once more. The bottom flaps of a tent flutters, catching my attention. A familiar blonde girl carrying a sack of fruit exits.

I gasp, startling a customer beside me. It can't be.

Molly.

I rush to her, nearly crashing at her feet. "Molly! It's me, Layla."

"Layla?" Her hand covers her mouth. Then she grips me into a hug. "It's you! Ever since you helped me that day, I never gave up."

"How are you here?"

" 'Eye for an eye.' Samuel told me how you broke your curse. He gave me a chance by keeping me safe each night. When I'd confessed to Mother what I'd done, I never went back to that blasted forest." Her chin trembles. "I sabotaged her relationship with a man she loved dearly. Told everyone he'd touched me. It never happened and he could never show his face. But when I spilled the truth, I was free. My curse broke, Layla. Just like yours. I'm free," she adds again, as if she's still comprehending.

"But what about Samuel? Where is he?"

Her lashes lower as she shakes her head softly. "Still trapped like the rest of 'em."

It's unfair.

She's here. I'm here. And he's not.

I shove past her. She catches my shoulder. "Wait. Where are you going?"

"How can you sit here shopping for fruit while Samuel remains trapped? If he's not free from that horrible curse, then neither am I. I won't stop 'til I break it."

"Layla." She reaches to grasp my hand. "You should know something. Samuel was weaker the last I saw him. His body was…different. It's like he was changing into something else. I don't know what's become of him now."

Her words paralyze me. I remember when I last saw him. She speaks the truth. He was shrinking, as if reverting back into a boy. Everything about him that helped him fight was dissipating.

"He's transforming back into a human," I announce.

"Why?"

"I don't know." I pause. "Maybe it has to do with all the lives he's saved."

Her brows pull together as if I'm speaking a foreign language. "That's not all. He's a target, Layla. He can't protect himself anymore, and the monsters have been relentlessly hunting him."

So now he's being punished for his good deeds. My head throbs as rage boils within me. What would happen if he were eaten again? Would he die? Or worse? Would he lose his morality, the piece of him that protected me and Molly?

"Molly, you can help me. Help me free Samuel." I reach for her hand. "A friend and I have a lead to help break his curse. And I could use another pair of eyes on this."

She pulls away, her hand gripping her arm. "I'm grateful to you and for what Samuel did. But I don't want to get sucked back into this. I want nothing to do with that awful curse. As long I'm truthful with myself, I'll never get cursed again."

She turns and disappears into the crowd.

"Molly—"

She's a coward. After what Samuel gave her, she won't even try to return the favor to him.

I trudge aimlessly, questioning my own motives. Maybe I shouldn't be quick to judge. Molly's just a little girl. She endured the same nightmare I had and managed to reach her freedom, and here I am acting as if her freedom doesn't matter—or worse, as if I would switch her for Samuel.

The truth is Samuel is in the same position I was in. But who will save him? Who will rush to his aid when he's cornered by those horrible beasts? Every piece of my heart deflates.

A hand lands on my shoulder, and I jump. I turn to see Mr. Alden.

"Layla, I think I found something. A former employee claims to know the grandson of Velma Blacknoc. The grandson runs and stays at Ana's Tavern."

My heart quickens. I pray it steers us on the right path, not a dead end.

Chapter Ten

Mr. Alden and I gather in the cramped, private quarters of Corey Blacknoc, three levels above the guests dining and mingling below. Their laughter and clinking of dishes reach us. The wooden walls and floor make it seem as if they have us trapped in a crate. One small bed and a desk holding a stick of candles occupy the space. I try hard not to fidget on the stool. The man across the room barely gives us ten seconds of his time.

The eighty-four-year-old Corey leans against the rickety desk with arms folded. His hands are rough and cracked. Gray hair has long ago covered his head. The only hint of his true color is the few black whiskers remaining in his scrubby white beard.

Corey's knuckles brush along his chin. "I never believed in it. Thought my grandmother just enjoyed telling scary stories."

Mr. Alden fills a spindle chair beside me. "One hundred and forty-one years ago, your grandmother, Velma Blacknoc, created the Blacknoc book. She must have known the answer to breaking the curse."

Corey raises a brow. "If I knew none better, I'd say you believe in it."

Mr. Alden stands. "It's real. I didn't believe it either, but then I saw it with my own eyes the curse snatch that girl out from thin air." He gestures at me. "Not to mention there are reports of kids going missing each year. Do you think those disappearances are coincidence?"

Corey eyes Mr. Alden. "From a librarian, I'd expected more. Why encourage the child?" He shakes his head at me. "If it's true, then explain why you're still standing here?"

Samuel. My missing hand. I tell him everything, and instead of staring in awe, his unperturbed expression holds nothing but doubt.

" 'Eye for an eye,' eh? I'd like to see this message for myself."

Mr. Alden huffs. "It's safe at the library. Look, we've come a long way. Will you tell us what you know?"

Corey takes a seat on a stool beside the bed that rubs against his dingy desk. "The story is nothing but ramblings from a crazy old hag. I barely even knew my grandmother. She died at ninety-one when I was nine. In the time I saw her, all she filled me with was stories of watching her sister Mara go mad with vengeance over the death of her son. Then mad from the curse itself. Black magic consumed Mara. Grandmother seemed eager to make sure I was always obedient so the curse wouldn't take me. Said I would opt out of being a prospect by the time I reached twenty. But you see, my mother never knew a Mara Blacknoc. Mara is fictional, a wild creation made up by my grandmother." He rolls his eyes and expels a heavy breath.

A visible shiver runs along Mr. Alden's shoulders. "Then tell us the fictional tale."

Corey taps the heel of his boot against the stool leg. "As my grandmother told it, Mara cut out the heart of her dead infant son, Ryan Blacknoc, so she could use it to create the curse. She wrapped the heart in one of his blankets and tied it with a bootie lace. A sacrificial devotion to keep the curse alive and powerful enough to last. 'A heart bound, traps the rotten, deep in the ground, left to be forgotten.' "

"A heart bound?" I repeat. "That's it!"

Mr. Alden looks at me as if I'd said something forbidden. He shakes his head. "That doesn't sound good."

I inch my seat toward Corey. "Do you know where Mara could have buried her son?"

The man half coughs and half chuckles. "I think I'm done entertaining you with this foolishness."

"No. Please, sir. Anything at all can help." I stand and inch close to him. "Please, if you tell me, I'll work for free at your tavern. Surely, you need someone to clean rooms. I can cook, too. And my grandfather is a hunter. I can provide you with delicacies from the forest."

He tilts his chin, considering for a second. "How early can you start?"

"When can you tell us what we need to know?"

****

Back at the library, Mr. Alden hurries to spread maps across the table in our regular meeting room. Lit candles line the walls and lanterns rest on top of loose books around us. He points at the ridge lines on a map.

"Corey said near the Del Rise Mountains. If that's where they supposedly burned Mara Blacknoc, maybe she would have buried her son near there."

I swallow. "So, all we have is an idea but not an exact location."

Mumbling under my breath, I plop on the chair. It

creaks under my weight. Corey didn't know the specific location. Just the name of mountains. That shred of info wasn't worth the weeks of work I'd have to do in his blasted tavern. I blow out a breath. I should be more grateful. It's more than we had yesterday. More than we've ever had.

"That's the least of our problems." Mr. Alden whips the side of his cloak behind him.

"What do you mean?"

"Those mountains are haunted."

"Why didn't Corey mention that?"

"Because he doesn't believe in that nonsense." The librarian neatly folds the maps and sticks them in a satchel across his chest. "Frankly, I'd be better off if I didn't believe in any of this foolishness."

"I've run from and fought monsters. I think I can handle ghosts."

Mr. Alden frowns. "Can't say the same for myself. I'm just a librarian, somehow stuck helping an adolescent girl."

"And I'm just an adolescent girl, grateful for this old man's help." I gesture at him with a smirk.

He grins and leaves the room to fetch more tools. When he returns, gear to keep us alive in the woods clink and scatter across the table.

I raise a brow at Mr. Alden. "I thought you were a librarian, not an explorer."

A quiet chuckle escapes him. "These are merely items I acquired over the years. At least they'll finally be of use."

Leaning back into my chair, I gather a breath and exhale it. "What if we don't find what we're looking for? What if it's another dead end?" I won't be able to stomach that despair again.

Mr. Alden packs more into his satchel and stuffs a bigger bag with a tent and cooking equipment. Then he pauses and sighs, meeting my gaze. "It is a possibility we may find nothing, but it's also possible we could end this curse for good. It's our choice to decide which to pursue, and we can only reach either outcome if we try."

He's right. I'm all for turning over every stone and searching the ends of the world to find the solution that will kill this curse. But time is also not on our side. What if it's already too late and Samuel is being eaten as I speak? I shake my head. *Can't think that way.* We need to keep moving. Keep searching.

****

I never thought I'd say it, but a part of me misses being a monster. Who would have thought being human was incredibly difficult for staying alive? At least my old form allowed me to protect myself and others. Now I'm worthless.

And I will have to run forever. The powerful paws that added a spring to my sprint are no longer there. The claws that once protruded out from my fingers are gone. Now I look like a man in need of nail filing. My fur and horns are gone. Tender skin covers my flesh. Exceptional hearing gone. My powers gone. Even that witch's voice is gone. I guess I'm no use to her, being human and all.

As I crouch in a ditch shielded by underbrush, Chasin, a boy I'd rescued days ago, walks up to me. I didn't even hear him. His short golden bangs stick to the top of his head. His eyes are slanted, giving the illusion that he's always smiling. Dirt smears his pants and arms.

Chasin bends over to pull off his trousers. Then he hands them to me to cover myself. "While I can't give you back your hide, this is the least I can do."

Since the transformation, I have had nothing to cover my nakedness. Running for my life, I never stopped to think about it. Maybe because I was no stranger to shame.

"Are you sure?" I ask.

Chasin remains in his undergarments. "Just put them on."

I nod and slip on the trousers. They are a tight fit but better than nothing. The boy's knees and shins are exposed. My heart breaks for him. Why would he bother to clothe me?

As if reading my mind, he answers, "A monster needs his armor to fight."

A grin forms on my lips. Beginning with Layla and Molly, a movement has formed. Kids band together and look after one other, including me, a former beast they see as their ally. But I don't see how I'm any use to them now.

Chasin looks into my gaze, searching for guidance. He doesn't appear older than eleven and seems to see me as his guardian. What could he possibly want from me? I can't keep him safe.

"I know what you did for her," he says

"You need to keep your voice down," I whisper.

"She must love you if you're the reason that girl is searching to break the curse."

My stomach sinks. "Who?"

He pauses. "Layla. There are rumors in town that she's trying to break the curse."

Waves crash into my chest as my breathing hitches. Just the sound of her name makes my heart flutter. She loves me? Could she care that much that she hasn't given up on me? I wouldn't give up on her either. After all this time, she hadn't forgotten about me. She's fighting against a curse that is no longer her concern.

I smile at him. "Layla's a real fighter. Stronger than me."

"Do you think she can actually break the curse?" Chasin whispers, hope obviously filling him.

I nod with a smirk. "Yes. And you better believe it too, kid." I peek over the rim of the ditch and listen. Then I motion to Chasin. "Stay with me."

I may be helpless, but I still know how these beasts think. They like to circle certain areas. On a map, it would look like a pattern of rings side by side in a triangle. They cover more ground this way, especially if they spread out into groups.

I lead Chasin down a narrow, damp path that softens our footfalls, careful not to scrape against the branches. I gesture for Chasin to do as I do. I study the direction of the wind. Our scent carries south, from which we came. There is no possible way for me to promise a monster isn't lurking behind us. All I can do is pray the path in front of us remains clear.

As soon as I find a few sturdy sticks, I make a spear and hand one to Chasin. Then I sharpen my own. I glance at the pointy tip.

"Eye for an eye." After Layla broke her curse, it occurred to me countless times that I could end my curse. A life for a life. The one I took. If I could take that dog's life as if it didn't matter, I could certainly take my own pathetic life.

But what of Chasin beside me? Or others like him? I'm no good to them if I'm dead. I shake my head, growling out of habit.

Chasin glances at me, his brows rising in question. As I turn away, something snags Chasin's boot. It pulls him through the brush and across the foliage as if he's a doll.

"No!" I dive for Chasin, but I'm too slow. A monster drags Chasin behind by his foot. Chasin's head and arms flail out of control. The beast speeds up until he is out of sight.

I stop to catch a breath. If only I had my old stamina back.

The monster must have stopped running too because I hear it slowly dragging my friend's body across the leaves. Panic laces Chasin's pleas for help. Pain turns his cries to high-pitched screams.

"Chasin!" My voice cracks.

I sprint but I don't know which direction to go. He could be anywhere, and I can't see past the broad trees. If I can hear Chasin's own flesh being torn apart, he can't be far. I try to follow the agonizing screams. Bones crunching under powerful teeth spin my head in all directions. The screams intensify. I freeze. More snapping of bone and flesh. Chasin's cries cut off. My heartbeat is loud in the silence.

Bile slams against the back of my throat. I bend down to stifle a scream.

There is nothing left for me do. All I can think of is to run, run away from the friend I failed to keep safe. My tongue bleeds under the gnashing of my teeth. A rustle stirs in the distance, snapping me back to focus. Something in the woods inches closer.

I set off to get as far as I can away from the area.

My thoughts scramble. It's my fault! I should have seen that beast coming, should have kept Chasin closer. I slump against a tree and plop onto my bottom. My head feels heavy in my palms. I stretch out my aching legs. Cuts mark my feet and face. Bruises cover my arms. If I could just heal myself maybe I could fight again.

Maybe I'm delusional, but I focus on the old wounds covering my body. I try to tell my body to heal itself.

"Please," I beg.

Nothing happens. I still ache and bleed like a human. My heel kicks the dirt. I rub the back of my neck. If I keep spilling my blood like this then I'm sure to be found and eaten. I can't tell what is worse, being human, or being a monster.

In a distance, flames flicker between trees. Shadows of bobbing heads make their way closer. A trio of kids emerge with spear-like torches, panting and sweating.

A girl points at me. "Which way did Chasin go?"

"It's too late," I mutter. "He's one of them now."

She dips her head and squeezes her eyes shut.

A lanky boy with shaggy, black hair kneels at my level. There's maturity in his gaze that I haven't seen in a while. "You're Samuel, right?"

I nod.

He extends a callous hand. "I'm Gabriel. Come on. We need you. Stay close and avoid the west trees over there." He points off in a distance. "Traps."

The rest of the night I follow the group. With more feet shuffling beside each other, we're much louder than I prefer.

A monster's ear-blistering yelp sounds at the other side of the woods.

One of the girls, Arabella, shoots Gabriel a knowing glance. "I bet that'll leave a deep mark."

I can't help but smirk along with the group. They're ruthless, evolved into a much-needed weapon to survive. In a sense, I feel one step behind them, as if I need to catch up to meet their strength.

Before we can move any farther, the sun rises. I'm relieved for the break. The group disappears like puffs of smoke, safe and back into their homes. To my horror, I long ago discovered that I don't join them but remain in the sunny forest. At least the monsters can't roam under the sun, but it's still not fair. I'm human now. Am I not even given the chance to return home, even for a short time? To see my father. To find Layla.

My body feels lost, like a coin stuck in a crack where no one will ever look.

I let the sun's rays soak into my skin, the warmth reminding me of Layla's breath on my face.

"Layla," I whisper. My heart aches. "Please find me."

I imagine Layla reaching out through my unseen prison walls. She's searching for me. I hold on to the image and can almost see her in the sunlight through the trees, Layla walking my way.

Find me.

Chapter Eleven

The wagon rocks as we traverse up the steep path. Mr. Alden grunts when we hit a bump. The cover of the forest will be our next stop to rest. No telling how long we will spend in the haunted woods. I hope a week's worth of gear will suffice. Mr. Alden had to find a quick replacement to tend to the library for a few days. I had to tell Grandfather I was taking a trip with friends to the Del Rise. He didn't object, which made me think he was glad to hear that I was socializing again.

Mr. Alden helps me off the wagon. Our two horses find water at a stream running along a shore of pebbles and dancing flowers. I shiver, fidgeting in my cloak against the cold wind. A full moon greets me. I have to remind myself the anxiety stirring in my chest is only pounding out of habit whenever night falls. I'm no longer cursed.

We make camp. The fire pops between me and Mr. Alden. I slurp my half of the carrot soup, inhaling the steam to melt my frozen lips.

Mr. Alden scratches the back of his head, then winces at the howls and shrieks of the wildlife. "We've been out here for three days, circled areas twice. I don't know what else we expect to find."

The doubt in his tone reinforces my uncertainty. "I'll know when we see it."

The librarian pulls out the map and examines it for

the hundredth time. “Do you think a sign will sprout out from the ground and say, ‘Please look here?’ ”

He’s tired. We both are. But it still doesn’t stop the sting. A tear wants to snake down my face. I tilt my chin.

I’d given up on Samuel once before. I refuse to do it again. It’s best to ignore Mr. Alden. I snuggle into my tent and close my eyes. Three days of only four hours of sleep each night weighs on me until slumber floats my subconscious into darkness.

Worms wriggling in the dirt flash across my mind. Faint whispering. The roar of Samuel bursting through my skull. More whispering. Then voices telling me to eat and choke on death.

Something caresses my ear. I jump up with a clammy back and frantic eyes. Slipping through the tent flaps, I glance around wildly. The stars and moon are still over me. The fire crackles strong between me and the shelter that Mr. Alden should be in. His tent door is open.

I dart inside, plucking the blankets for a sign of his whereabouts.

My heart races. “Mr. Alden?”

The horses by the wagon shift, their nostrils rigid and necks stiff. No sign of Mr. Alden there either. No evidence hinting of his location.

Nothing.

My breathing quickens. What if an animal took him? I can’t lose another friend. I have to get him back.

Fixing a torch, I set on a path that has barely any footprints. The impressions are odd, as if toes dragged across them. A breeze whips through my cloak, and I pull it back across my chest as I slip through dense brush. Branches snag on my hood. I shove on, not caring about the holes ripping into my garment.

A twig snaps.

I pause and listen. Boots crunching foliage makes me twirl around. The torch sprays light across a dark figure. My eyes squinting, I raise the torch.

Mr. Alden stands perfectly erect, his chin dipped and avoiding eye contact.

"Mr. Alden?"

With a hollow scream, he charges me, his arms flailing until they get a hold of my shoulders and shove me down. I land on the ground with a grunt. Mr. Alden's strength might as well be a bear smothering me.

My one hand and stub do nothing to push him off. His hand grips my neck, while the other grabs a scoop of dirt to smear across my face.

In a whisper he says, "Monster. Monster."

I scream, trying to turn my head away. "Mr. Alden please! Stop!"

The torch knocked out of my hand burns hot beside me. He leaves me no choice. I grab the torch and press the flame into his arm. A small flame crawls up Mr. Alden's sleeve and he lurches off me, yelling. He drops and rolls until the fire extinguishes.

His terrified gaze meets mine, his jaw slack and lower lip trembling. "Oh God, what have I done? I-I'm so sorry. I don't know what came over…" He rubs the sweat off his forehead.

"What just happened?" I bark.

"Something was inside of me. Told me to do awful things." His head tilts, as if he's listening to something. He rushes toward me and helps me up. "We need to get out of here. Now. We're going home. This place is…" Something snaps a few feet away and he stills. "It's not right. Let's go." He pulls me his way.

I jerk free. If only he knew what he hears out here is nothing compared to the chaos I'd dealt with every night with Samuel.

"No," I snap. "We're close to something. I feel it."

"Close to evil, that's what." The librarian tries to reach for my hand, but I step back. "Layla, please. We shouldn't disturb any sinister spirits that lurk here."

I'd run against evil. Came face to face with it. Was taken by it. Even became it. The old man I'd hurt returns to me, and I wince. And I know I can't run from evil now. I have to confront it.

"This is where I need to be. Don't you see? Evil is what we're looking for. I will find it and I will stop it. For Samuel."

I round him and retrace the path back to camp. The horses neigh at our appearance. Mr. Alden catches up.

"I am in charge of you, and I say we head home."

I pat the black horse's neck, his strong breathing steadying my nerves. His name is Hubert. "Then go back. I can do this on my own."

He shakes his head and puts his hands on his hips. "I won't leave without you. What would your grandfather say?"

After untying Hubert from the wagon, and fastening a small lantern to my belt, I awkwardly pull myself up onto the horse by his mane.

Mr. Alden grabs my leg. "What do you think you're doing, girl?"

"I'm sorry, but I won't leave without Samuel. Heeya!" I jam my heels into Hubert's sides, and he takes off, leaving Mr. Alden behind. His steadily fading voice demands my return.

But I can't. Not when I'm this close.

****

The monster at my heels is the latest addition. Chasin. There is a hint of gold fur on top of his head, and his black eyes are slightly slanted. A piece of undergarment is still stuck in his fur in his inner thigh. I'm tempted to turn around and tell him to stop. It's me, Samuel. But I know it won't do me any good. He's gone, trapped deep in that monstrous body, overrun by the curse.

Without my strength and powers, too many beasts are taking form each night. It's become impossible to escape them alone.

I must find the others. Survive. We're stronger together. I make a sharp turn between trees that Chasin can't fit through.

On the other side is another snarling beast waiting for me. Josh. But is it? I almost don't recognize him.

My eyes widen. Impossible. How did he change, too? He's become even worse. His horns are longer. Shoulders bulkier. His eyes glow brighter, almost deep crimson. Even his fangs are pointier. My heart shoots up my throat.

Then I remember Josh has eaten more kids than I can count. Can it be he's graduated to an ultimate killer? A point with no return?

Josh takes a swipe at me with his massive claws. I roll to the side behind a log, but I'm not fast enough. Claws nick my side. I moan, holding my bloody torso. Chasin comes from behind to block me. No! I'm surrounded.

I hear barking in the distance. The monsters stop in their tracks, their ears erect as if curious dogs themselves. With all my might, I use my momentum to roll down a slope. Gravity pulls me away from the beasts. I'm grateful for the fall.

My body tumbles and rolls until it slams into water. I sink as bubbles escape my mouth. A cloud of red surrounds me. I kick up. My head surfaces and I gasp.

I'm in a massive lake, almost a bowl-shape. At the rim are hundreds and hundreds of monsters watching me. My heart feels punctured, and I'm bleeding internally. Roars of war erupt.

There's no doubt this is personal, as if it's the curse getting back at me. I've never seen so many monsters in all my time in the forest. A handful look like Josh, their glowing eyes piercing through mine. I feel their powerful paws from here as they kick dirt behind them.

Barking sounds again. I whirl around. In the center of the lake is a little island. A large chocolate dog stands on it. Floppy ears bounce as the dog paces. The dog pauses. He stares right at me. *It can't be*. I must be seeing things. But the dog barks once more. It wants my attention.

The noise seems to tick off the army of monsters. They roar in unity and charge into the lake after me.

There's nothing I can do but swim toward that dog. I kick my legs and toss my arms one after the other, the water stinging the wound on my torso. The beasts close in on me. The barking grows frantic. The dog dips his head and shoulders down, his tail wagging behind him. I don't know why but I must reach him. Almost there.

I pull up halfway on the island, and the dog meets

me. He lowers his head, and I wrap my arms around his thick neck. The beating heart in his chest feels like an anchor steadying me. His gentle presence swarms me. I relax against his soft fur. I'm grateful for the second chance he gave me. The powers I once wielded. My freewill. Without him, I wouldn't have been able to rescue Layla or the others.

I whisper into his floppy ear. "I'm so sorry for what I did to you. I accept my fate."

The warmth of the dog steadies my trembling limbs, and I squeeze tighter to smother the fear beginning to drown me. The dog licks my ear.

Strong claws hook into my legs and yank me down. I howl as I release the dog, so it won't follow me into the murky water. It doesn't belong in the place I'm going.

Chapter Twelve

Hubert gallops through the forest at full speed, the treetops casting shadows that run over our heads. The power of his hooves pounds the dirt but doesn't compare to the drumming in my ears.

I don't even know where I'm going.

Tugging on the reins, I stop Hubert and take a deep breath, listening. For something. Anything.

Dead silence haunts the forest. A shiver runs up my back, one that even Hubert seems to absorb because he backs up. I readjust him to the trail. He balks.

That's it. All I must do is follow the cold sensation gripping my spine, and the trail the horse dreads. The one that seems to be the darkest. The one that projects malice.

My chest pounds. My mouth goes dry, and the hairs on every inch of my body stand on end. Hubert tries to shift away again, but I reposition him.

"Heeya! Go!"

He dashes down the wicked path. Each step he takes makes me feel as though I'm sinking further and further into mud. A pull to my right tells me I should avoid that direction. So I guide Hubert into the threat. Nausea pummels my stomach. Everything in my gut tells me I shouldn't be here.

The dense wood squeezes tighter and tighter. I have no choice but to dismount and leave Hubert. As I untie my lantern from my belt, I guide the light out as far as I can in front of me. Branches scrape my face. Cuts mark my cheeks. The dirt Mr. Alden smeared into my face seeps into my cuts, stinging me.

A wave of fear pounds me. It never occurred to me that I could get lost in this forest. Adrift near the Del Rise Mountains and never seen again. What good am I to Samuel then?

A haunting whisper freezes me in my tracks. Wild winds pick up, shoving the brambles that surround me back and forth. Further scratching my skin and itching my stub.

Listening, I follow the faint whisper. It takes me across the thicket and into a small glade. The tree line circles an area where a tumbled chimney lays buried in weeds. Part of a home, maybe?

Gravel crunches under my boots as I scan my surroundings with my light. Nothing but chipped chimney stone, mostly swallowed by nature. The stench of ash remains but there are no signs of a fiery aftermath.

I straighten, glimpsing a shadow darting into the forest. My pulse drives forth. Even a girl with a death wish would turn back. But I follow the shadow, shoving through foliage.

"Here," a whisper calls.

I rotate, meeting a ghostly figure shimmering right in front of me. Gasping, I fall to the ground and scramble back, grip shaking on the handle of the lantern. The fog-like figure with little expression squats to my level. I crawl back until a tree stops me.

"Layla?" it moans.

All the blood drains from my face. Its transparent

face barely shows a pointed nose or cheek bones. Indentions where eyeballs should be make me feel like I'm staring into an abyss.

"H-how do you know me?"

"I've seen you in visions. Longed for you to be the one to free me. It's why I gave Samuel his second chance." The tone is inviting, even omnidirectional.

"Who are you?" I demand, trying to sound unruffled.

"Ryan Blacknoc."

The blood drains from my face. My throat shrivels. I can't seem to find my voice. Every word, which sounds more like the shy voice of the wind, paralyzes me.

"You're the witch's son?" I force myself to say. "Mara Blacknoc's son?"

He nods.

"But that can't be," I continue. "Mara's son was an infant when he died." This apparition stands at a man's height. He speaks.

"Mara cursed me this way. An infant could never do the work I do every day to keep the curse alive. That's why I'm in this form. My mother insisted upon it."

Using the tree for support, I try my best to stand. But my legs wobble, ready to buckle. The same chill I'd felt with Mr. Alden returns. The ghost rises, his shimmering body seemingly ready to blow away.

"You need to hurry," Ryan snaps. "She doesn't like revisiting this place, but it doesn't always stop her. Go now. Free us all."

"Stop who?"

"My mother," he growls. "Mara. You must end

her."

"Can't you do something, like how you helped Samuel?"

"I only interfered with Samuel. I saw the slightest crack in Mara's curse and a strong candidate who could carry out my wish. My only hope was that Samuel would remain strong enough without Mara's influence. And he did. He brought you." There is a smile in Ryan's tone, but it quickly fades. "Now you must end this."

"But how?"

"You see, I *am* the Blacknoc Curse, the only thing keeping this curse alive. You must find and destroy my heart. Remove the worms of death and then burn the heart."

My brows pull inward. " 'Worms of death?' "

"Yes. It is the only thing that will break my mother's curse. The worms of her flesh guard my heart. Nothing on earth can remove them but the one willing to accept each sting." His voice thickens. "Removing them comes at a high price. Once the toxins from their stings have worked into your body, it will slowly eat at your heart, and you will eventually die. 'Heart for heart.' "

That's it. The final clue. "Eye for an eye, and heart for a heart." But he's suggesting that I die.

Would I die? To break the curse? To end Samuel's pain?

I shake my head, trying to process Ryan's words.

A deafening shriek from a woman erupts around us. The wind carries the echo for miles as if she's everywhere at once, lurking behind each tree.

Ryan curses. "You need to go now."

My legs freeze.

He points at a hidden trail spiraling closer to the mountains. "Follow that and count eighty steps, then make a sharp right. You can't miss it. If you get lost, follow my four-legged friend."

His apparition shimmers. Behind him a faint green silhouette storms around the trees angrily and flies toward us.

I sprint to the path. Daring a glance over my shoulder, I see the apparitions of Ryan and Mara collide like bucks fighting. What sounds like lightning striking a tree booms across the forest. A woman, who I can only assume is Mara, howls. Her screams reach out, as if she's right behind me.

Shoving the lantern in front of me, I dash across the trail, almost forgetting to count the eighty steps.

Eleven.

Twelve.

Another shriek. Then something, like a fist, slams into my spine. I crash on my palm with a yelp. A flash of green flies by. I'm reminded of my fight against the monsters in the forest. Fury ignites inside me. I growl and scramble upright, running on the path again.

Forty.

Fifty.

Almost there.

The green phantom snakes in between trees, her maniacal screeches piercing my eardrum. She must know what I will do. But even *I* don't know what I'm doing.

Ryan's words haunt me. *Remove the worms of death.*

When I ran from the monsters each night with

Samuel, it always felt as if death were only a few feet behind me. Now it's here, right in front of me, and I'm running straight toward it.

Samuel's words return to me. *I believe no matter how awful we are, we all deserve another chance.*

Samuel gave me my second chance, and I am his only hope. I'm the only person who can free him. Tears spring from my eyes. The storm of darkness could have easily blown me over, but Samuel was there to shield me from the torrents of evil.

Seventy.

Eighty.

I make a sharp right, but I see nothing but a slope. Another fist slams into my back. I tumble down the steep grade. Moaning, my vision blurs. I lost the trail. Where has that witch led me?

With one hand and a stub, I stand and try to refocus. I grab my cracked lantern. Scanning the uneven terrain does me no good. Where am I?

A figure stands in the shadows, watching me. I gasp as it steps closer into view, my chest tightens. *No. It's not real.* Yet the old man remains as real as my trepidation. He stands unmoving, his right hand still gone. I blink. And then blink again. But he's still there.

"You. Did this to me," he moans.

But he's a mute. He can't speak

"You. Took it from me." His right stub of hand quivers, shooting currents of chills across my back.

"I am so sorry," I mutter repeatedly.

"Monster!" His voice distorts to a near animal-like growl. He lifts his left hand and points at me, then points at the ground near my feet.

I glance down. Something pokes out from the dirt.

I kick at it to unveil a cut-off, withered hand. I scramble back. The old man's hand! My gut churns. This isn't real. I claw at my face to rub my eyes. He's not really here.

I look up. The man is gone. My breath catches as I scan the area. Not even footprints. That witch is toying with me. I can't let her get to me. But I don't know where else to go. I lost the trail I was supposed to be on thanks to her.

The echo of barking jolts me forward. What dog would be out here? It's another trick.

A chocolate dog emerges from the brush and dips his front half, his bottom sticking up with a wagging tail. He barks and barks as if wanting me to follow him. Didn't Ryan say if I got lost to follow his four-legged…friend?

Oh, please let it be so! I motion toward the dog. He turns to lead me down another path. The dog is so fast I can barely keep up. I can hardly see him and must rely on the barking alone to guide me.

"Layla."

I whirl at the sound of my name. A young man stands there. There is something familiar in his gaze.

"Samuel?"

"Layla! It's me. I broke my curse. The dog brought me here."

A warm smile forms on his lips. He's as human as I'd ever seen him. Smooth, clean face. Sandy eyes match his short, wavy hair. All I want to do is wrap my arms around him.

My heart leaps as I race toward him but stop midway. *Eye for an eye.* How could he have broken his own curse? That would have required him to take his own life. Barking sounds in the distance, snapping me out of my daze.

"No. It's not you."

The shadows on his face move, as if they're twisting his features into a snarling wolf. He's transforming into the monster I first met.

"It is me, Layla." A wicked smirk pulls his lips up, revealing pointy fangs. "Don't you recognize me?"

Claws shoot out from his furry paws. His limbs bend and snap into thick muscular legs. Samuel gets down on all fours and curls his drooling lips. His glassy eyes spark with rage. Samuel charges me. I turn to sprint. Heart pounding, I search for the barking.

Woof!

There! It leads me straight into dense trees. Before I can take another step, a powerful jaw clamps down on my boot. Then it yanks me back. I fly through the air. I hit the ground on my side and roll across the weeds, nicking my cheeks on the thorns in the process.

I whimper, feeling as if a mountain just slammed into me.

Samuel leaps at me. His front paws land on my arms, pinning me to the ground. I yelp. Sheer power presses me down. I fight back tears. Samuel pulls his lips back into a smirk.

"I've been wanting to spill your blood for a while now," he says. His hot breath sweeps over my face.

"The real Samuel would never hurt me." Rough paws continue to dig into my skin.

"You don't know what Samuel is capable of."

"I know enough, Hag. He's strong. Stronger than you." I growl.

Samuel roars, drizzling my face with drool. I pray

the witch can't truly harm me. In death, she must be limited. Otherwise, I would have long been dead.

I dare to let my tongue run wild. "You're weak. You couldn't stop Samuel. And you can't stop me."

Samuel shakes his head with a snort. He extends his jaw. Then he lurches for my face. I squeeze my eyes shut. Something slimy with ridges passes through my face, momentarily cutting off my air supply.

I gasp. Samuel is gone.

A fit of howls erupt. I get to my feet and scan the area. No sign of Samuel. Relief and anger flood me. It's just Mara, messing inside my head. I set my jaw. Mara wants to collapse my mind. She failed to do so in the forest with the real Samuel. She certainly won't accomplish that now. I'll make her stop. Forever.

Emerging from the trees, I enter a small clearing. All the treetops claw toward the center, toward the tombstone resting there. That must be it. I thrust out my lantern. The light sprays on the engraving that reads: *Ryan Blacknoc Rest Not Until The Wicked Have Fallen.*

Something slams into my side, knocking the air out of me. I drop the lantern. It shatters on the ground. I hiss as a shimmering green glow paces the area. Mara vanishes, for now.

Time to end this.

As I scramble to the tomb, screams reverberate in the distance. I dig into the earth with my hand and stub. The hard soil slices my fingertips, but I keep going. Whispering surrounds me. I make out the voice. Samuel.

He stands on the other side of the tomb, back in human form. "Please don't do this, Layla."

My nose wrinkles. "You foolish crone. I grow

bored of your childish tricks."

Samuel's face twists in disgust and his form condenses into smoke that disappears. Clawing at the dirt, I shout, trying to overpower the surrounding whispering.

A piece of blue fabric pokes out. I scoop my fingers into the small pit to pull it out of the ground. A bootie lace fastens something inside the fabric.

This is it. Ryan's blanket.

I tear the lace and unfold the blanket. The stench of rotten flesh punches me. A cluster of worms cover a small object. An armor of thin spines shrouds the vibrant orange worms. The tips of the spines are black. I yelp, dropping it on the ground. The impact doesn't shake the worms off. The creatures are not ordinary. What fresh hell spat these out? Panic smothers me.

The air carries another sibilant murmur. Like the howling wind, the whisper erupts to ear blistering screams.

"Layla, stop!"

I reel, my eyelids peeling wide. "Grandfather?"

Grandfather makes his way toward me. His arms open just like they always do right before I run into his embrace for a tight, protective hug. My throat is hollow. My knees weak. He pauses as if an invisible wall stands between us.

"Layla. It's time to come home. Come on. You're safe." He motions for me. "Let me take you home."

The comfort in Grandfather's voice tugs at my heart. But I know he's nothing more than a ghost of his image. I close my eyes tight. When I reopen them, I stare down at the spiny worms surrounding what can only be Ryan's heart. My chest pumps up and down as I attempt to push off their rigid bodies with a stick, but it's no use. They're seemingly glued in place.

The person taking my grandfather's form stands there. His tone spews venom. "You would save that murderer?"

"Yes. He isn't like that anymore."

He utters in two voices. "Liar. Wicked. Putrid."

"Are you paying attention, Mara?" I won't address this figure taking my grandfather's form anymore but direct my words all around me to that coward witch. "I don't want you to miss this."

My grandfather vanishes, and a taut, feminine voice emerges. Mara's words I assume. "You can't outrun the Blacknoc Curse."

Ignoring her, I shove a handful of dry grass on the faint fire where my shattered lantern had fallen. The tinder sets it ablaze. I try to smother the worms with the flames, but they will not burn. Impossible. Instead, the fire singes my stub. I shriek and jerk away. Mara's laugh stirs in a circle of echoes. Sweat slicks down my cheeks. Again, I try, but the fire is no longer my ally and will not hurt them.

Everything about these worms is evil and gut twisting. They're part of the curse. The only way to be rid of them is to do what Ryan said. Remove them by hand. Receive their stings. Then die.

Mara's words return. "You monster! Burn. You all will burn in hell with me."

"No." Cupping the heart in my hand, I rise. "Not all monsters are monstrous. We are now the threatening force." I take one last glance at the worms. "And your destroyer."

Wailing pierces my eardrums.

For Samuel. For every kid cursed. And for Ryan. Cradling the heart in the fold of my arm, I pluck each worm. Pricks penetrate my skin. Fire surges to my fingertips and down my arms. Small spots of blood drip from my fingers. The pricks remind me of the way Samuel's hide hurt me. I remember who I'm doing this for. I swallow a yelp and continue to pluck away the worms.

Mara screams, shaking the treetops as if she wants the branches to collapse on me. I pinch the last worm and it nearly leaves a hole on my fingertip. Adrenaline numbs the pains. What's left is a beating heart resting in my palm. Ryan's heart. I kick at the broken lantern to anger the fire. The flames escape and engulf the nearest foliage. I raise the heart above my head.

Mara shrieks. Gritting my teeth, I slam the heart down into the fire.

"No!" Mara cries.

The heart explodes into a cloud of green smoke, which swirls in the air like a storm. I dash back. The smoke grows bigger and bigger. In a deafening boom, it explodes into a wave, ripping through each blade of grass and tree. I stumble and fall on my bottom. The smoke disappears into the horizon.

I take a breath, rising to stand.

Silence.

Absolute peace reaches me. The air is lighter. The trees vigorous. The shadows subordinate to the guiding sky.

****

The sun ascends and I with it. Instead of the pack of monsters that once surrounded me, boys and girls stand in place. Chasin steps up behind me, creeping closer as if approaching a ghost. His human appearance knocks the breath out of me. I step back, hesitant of his actions. Then guilt gnaws me. Surely, he must be furious at me for failing to keep him safe. The sound of his flesh and bones tearing comes back to me.

"Samuel, it's me." He grins, taking a step forward.

I smile at him, gripping his bony shoulders to pull him into a hug. He returns the gesture and squeezes me.

"I'm back," he says in wonder. "But how?"

I pull away and ruffle his hair. "Layla. Has to be." She did it. She actually did it.

A weight I never knew I carried lifts off my chest. It's too good to believe. I had imagined this moment night after night. I fear if I blink it will all vanish.

The monsters are gone. Everyone is back to their true form. But Josh is not here. Shouts of joy erupt all around, like war cries after a battle won. I join them until my throat aches. The curse is over, but it's still hard to accept the scene around me.

I scan the crowd once more for Josh. He was one of the advanced monsters. Had it been too late for him? Was he…dead?

A hand rests on my shoulder. I turn to face Gabriel and pull him into a tight hug.

"She did it," he says, his voice half cracking.

I pull away and grip the sides of his face. "You bet she did."

A girl pumps her fist in the air. "Layla!"

"Layla." Another one shouts and repeats over and over.

"Layla. Layla." Gabriel joins in.

Soon, the whole bunch starts chanting her name over and over. Their hero.

Scanning the joyous crowd, I drink in the magnitude of Layla's victory. Swallowing hard, I grin. I must find that girl and thank her every day of my life. Forever devote my protection to her.

Bumping shoulders, I make my way through the crowd.

"Horns are gone," a boy says. "Human at last!"

Similar conversations follow as most are already making their way across the forest toward the nearest village. Emerging from the forest, I stand in awe. Everyone spreads along the tree line, the familiar sight of civilization. I drink in the view. People walk along the dirt trail. Some tend to gardens. Horses graze within fenced pastures. Birds sing and perch on the straw rooftops. A lump in my chest forms out of anticipation. How I ached to see it once more. Freedom.

One by one, everyone scatters. I don't see most until I reach my home village, Chanbyrde. Families reunite with their long-lost children. Boisterous laugher and joy fills the air like pollen spreading from flower to flower. Talk of a curse and monsters load the ears of the parents. With similar stories, I can't help but wonder if the parents have no choice but to believe their explanation for disappearing.

I seek one home in particular. On the outskirts of the village, a familiar man rakes a garden by his cottage. My heart swells. His back faces me, but I still recognize him. I never believed this moment would happen. Only in my dreams I would see him again. Now, he stands in the flesh. Layla gave this back to me. I want to rush over and hug him and never let go, but my feet feel as they are weighed down by rocks.

As I take a step forward, I'm surprised by my

nerves forcing my stomach into flips. I know and love this man, and yet I'm scared of what's to come. What will he think when he sees me? I don't know how long it's been. Judging by the new silver streaks running along the back of his head, I'd say three or four years. Maybe more.

I glance at myself in a puddle. But I still look the same. Eighteen. The curse must've stopped me from aging. What will Father say?

When I find the strength, I stroll up to the man.

"Father?"

He turns. His jaw goes slack, and his grip slips on the rake. It slaps to the ground beside him.

"Samuel?" He pales.

"It's me. I'm home, Father."

Tears leak from his eyes and he rushes to wrap his arms around me. I breathe in his familiar musky scent mingled with sweat and dirt, the one I'd known ever since I was a babe. His loss for words is replaced with sobs. He squeezes me tighter as if something will take me. I return the hug, my own throat clogged and incapable of forming words.

****

Father thought me insane when I told him the truth. The curse, and what I was. But it seems a part of him no longer cares what comes out of my mouth. He's just overjoyed to have me back. I couldn't be happier myself, but I am far from my true home. I need to find Layla. I know she is the very reason I returned to Father today.

When I tell Father I must leave, it takes convincing for him to let me go, even for a short time. I explain about Layla and why I must find her. Father is reluctant, but then agrees with me and sees me off.

Bouncing with the movement of my horse, I search Grutchburg City, trying to locate a library. Layla mentioned one here.

Spotting the engraved words *Grutchburg City Library* along the top of a building, I climb the stairs and pull on the doors with the letters G and L. They don't budge. I pound and shout, but no one answers.

Hurrying down the steps, I search the city, asking anyone for a dark-headed girl that goes by Layla Marlowe. No one knows. No one gives me a second look. Everyone is distracted with the phenomenon of the long-lost kids returning to their parents.

The dead ends prompt me to try another city. Another night won't descend without her. I will find her.

My pulse beats frantically as I explore Rydmont City. Crowds gather in the streets. Most celebrate the return of their children. Talk centers around a festival to celebrate "The Returned," as they call them, taking place in two days.

Layla must be here. If only I could track her down like I'd done in the forest. I long for her autumn scent, to touch her without puncturing her skin.

I inch closer to a massive fountain, the focal point of the city. It boasts a centerpiece sculpture of a swan spouting water from its mouth. The stream curves down like a transparent curtain. Extended wings drip over the rim as a divide from the front and back halves of the fountain. The swan shoots a powerful spray, and when the water falls back down, I see her standing on the opposite side behind the swan's wing.

Layla.

She scans the crowd, as if searching for someone. She seems lost. Her long black hair sways. Her brown skin is like the richness of the soil. I want to touch her. The curve of her chin draws my gaze to her lips, curved down in distress.

"Layla!"

Shoulders bump into mine as I scramble toward her, nearly tripping over the tip of the extended wing. Her back turns to me. She's walking away. I nearly lose sight of her dark head as I continue to push forward. More shoulders slam into mine. People shoot me glances as if I am the rudest brute they'd ever seen, but I don't care.

"Layla!" I roar.

She spins at the sound of her name, meeting my gaze. I reach her. Our chests are mere inches apart. Her gaze runs over me. Recollection floods them, and my heart is seized.

"Layla."

"Samuel!" My name on her lips nearly drops me to my knees. I feel her right stub rub against my spine as she embraces me and wince. She'd surrendered the hand willingly, but I was the one who took her hand. "I was so scared I'd never get another chance to see you again."

I move to kiss her cheek. Then my lips find hers, and she doesn't resist.

My heart aches, a good pain I never thought I'd feel or want. I can hold her without hurting her. I can breathe her in without worrying about a monster lurking behind her. But then I pull away enough to check, just out of habit.

Many folks pass us before we part.

Her cheeks are wet, and she shoves her head into my chest, weeping.

"Hey, everything is okay now." I cup her soft cheek and stretch my thumb up to wipe the tears away. "You saved me."

I dip my forehead and gently press it against hers.

She pulls away. A distinct flash of fear runs across her features. My gut turns.

"What's wrong?" I ask.

"I did something." Her voice thickens as her lower lip trembles. "It was the only way to break the curse. To save you and bring you back into my arms." Layla runs her left hand down the side of my face and to my shoulder. "And I don't regret a thing."

I feel the blood drain from my face. "What did you do?"

Everything spills from her in sobs. Ryan. Mara. The worms. She doesn't know how long she has left with me.

I embrace her again, fighting back angry tears. We sit on the damp edge of the fountain, squeezing each other. Her body trembles against mine as the swan shoots water once more to sprinkle us. Why would she do this to herself? Why end her life for mine?

Her warm body presses against mine as I hug her tighter.

As if somehow it will keep her away from death.

Chapter Thirteen

It was the only way. Layla's words haunted me. I thought our nightmares were over. That we could live happily. How foolish I was to think about such fantasies.

Through the window, I watch Layla awkwardly sweep the floors in Ana's Tavern. She pauses to rub her stub. I grit my teeth. Customers sit at tables with drinks in front of them. Laughter and chatter spill out of the tavern. Layla wipes sweat from her brow. My lips twist into a grimace as my fist rests on the window frame.

Instead of celebrating our freedom, Layla is stuck working her shift hours for Corey Blacknoc. I curse as I lean against the wooden pillar of the tavern. Layla should be spending her time with her grandfather. Not working like a dog in her fragile state.

Folks crowd the streets. Many still gather and praise the returned children.

Images of Layla dying in front of me plagues my gut. Trepidation surges through me as I try to control my thoughts, but slowly my world falls apart around me. I can't lose Layla like this.

I make my way inside, pushing the creaking door aside and stepping into a full room. One woman in a long skirt serves a tray of drinks to a table of four gabby men. I move closer. An antler chandelier holding candles at the tips hangs above me. Layla is off to the right. Not seeing me, she takes the broom into a room stacked with barrels.

"My nephew is one of the returned," a man at a table says. He sips his mug.

A woman sitting across from him says, "Where did all the children go to?"

Another gentleman beside her shrugs. "Probably a bunch of ungrateful brats who ran off, then came back after realizing it wasn't so easy out there on their own."

"For that amount of years?" the woman says. "I highly doubt it. Something or someone happened to them."

"The logic of a woman," he says.

The men laugh as the woman stares into her lap.

I shake my head. These people wouldn't dare laugh if I stood in my monster form before them. Not entertaining the idea any further, I make my way to the bar at the back of the tavern. An old man behind the bar works a rag inside an empty mug. Corey, I presume. I let out a heavy sigh as I squeeze between two customers.

"What can I get for you?" Corey asks.

"A cure for breaking the Blacknoc Curse."

Corey stops rubbing the rag in the mug and looks up at me. "Not another one of you."

"You remember Layla? The girl working for you in exchange for the information you gave her. 'A heart bound, traps the rotten, deep in the ground, left to be forgotten.' Sound familiar?"

Corey slings his rag over his shoulder. "I knew I should have never entertained you people with that tale."

"She found that special heart. Now, Layla is

marked for death."

He stands in disbelief and lets out a chuckle. His attention draws away to a customer asking for a drink.

"Please," I say again. "Layla broke the Blacknoc Curse for me and the others who were cursed. She's paying a fatal price for her sacrifice." I lower my voice, noting a woman on a stool raising a brow at me. "She can't die. Not like this. You have to help her."

"As I told your librarian friend, I'm no longer entertaining anyone with that ridiculous tale. My grandmother is dead, and that damn tale needs to die with her. Now, either you order a drink, or you leave."

I slam my fist on the bar top, startling the woman beside me and she skitters off.

I growl. "Listen, you old sack of bones. Layla is dying. I need to know how to cure her."

Corey flicks his wrist and snaps his fingers. Within seconds, strong hands grip my arms. A man with a beard covering most of his lips and chin towers behind me. He quickly pulls me away from the bar.

"Good day, sir," Corey says.

I squirm and kick. The man's grip on my arms squeezes tighter. He guides me toward the door.

"Let me go," I shout.

My chest hits the door as the man shoves me out and throws me onto the cobblestone street.

"Wait!" Layla calls from inside.

She bursts through the door and dives for me.

"What were you thinking?" She grips my arm, then helps me stand.

"I wanted answers from Corey."

"And did you get any?" Her sarcastic tone perturbs me. Being thrown out didn't sting as much as her hopelessness.

"No, but I will."

"Just stop." She stands and turns to go back inside.

I reach for her shoulder and make her face me. "How can you go back in there? Working for him nonetheless."

"Because it was my choice. I'm okay with the choice I made to save you."

"It's my choice not to lose you, and I'm not going to stop."

"Don't give me hope." A tear bubbles at the corner of her eye. "Don't give me hope that I could remain with you."

I pull her into a hug. Her breath is heavy against my ear. I inhale her.

"Don't expect me to ever stop. You are still mine to protect."

****

The passing weeks plunge by like the invisible nails pushing through my skull. Layla sits beside me at the healer's home. To my surprise, Layla's health is as good as I'd ever seen it. Her spirits are high. The smile on her lips doesn't fade.

I tested her this morning when I asked her to race me around her grandfather's property on horseback, her giggles and laughter still carrying my feet for miles. It made this visit more bearable.

Layla reaches for my hand and grasps it. She gives it a squeeze. I wink at her and then glance back at the woman sitting across from us.

The healer we are seeing lifts a bowl to her nose. The long table between us separates the stench from us. The woman doesn't wince when she inhales. Instead, she smiles. The healer reaches for the second bowl on the table and sniffs it.

Layla's palm sweats in my hand. The healer's pack of children run wild above us on the second floor. Their tiny feet add to the thrumming in my chest. I wish for silence at a time like this. My knee bounces. I want to reach across this table and demand the woman hurry.

Layla squeezes my hand once more. I glance at her and smile. I am supposed to give *her* comfort.

"You're not sick," the healer says.

Somehow, the bowl of Layla's urine and blood on the table proves Layla is healthy.

"Here," the healer says. "If you're still uncertain, take this."

Layla reaches for a bowl of yellow lentil soup. She sips it.

"How can you be sure?" I ask, leaning forward.

The healer gets up to mash herbs on the workbench behind her. "If you have your doubts, you can try these," she says over her shoulder.

When she returns to the table, she hands Layla a cup of an orange liquid consistent with dirt-like clumps. Layla inhales it and gags.

"This will heal any sickness or inflammation you may have within," the healer says.

And with that, Layla downs the cup. A burp escapes her.

"Pardon me." Layla's cheeks turn crimson.

I chuckle. "How do you feel?"

"I don't know. How am I supposed to feel?" She glances at the woman.

"Allow a few weeks and you should know if any sickness has subsided or not. If you still believe you are ill, I recommend you seek a priest."

Layla smiles. Hope fills her eyes while doubt plunges into the pit of my stomach. Am I the fool for bringing her here? For convincing her this would help? Was herb tea any match against a century-old curse?

Layla turns to face me. She leans over and wraps her arms around me. Her hot breath warms my neck.

"It's going to be okay," she says. "I can feel it."

I'm not sure if the purpose of her optimism is to shut out the doubts in my head, or her head. I return the hug, rubbing her back. For our sake, I hope she is right.

Chapter Fourteen

Once I return to my routine, finishing my chores and spending the evenings with Samuel, I feel a balance in my heart that I'd never thought I'd have again. Not a shred of my strength diminishes over the next passing months. I go about my days like I used to. A hint of normality slowly returns to my life.

The only reminder of the curse I was quick to forget is Samuel, who watches me like a hawk every day for signs of the curse. If I so much as sneeze, Samuel takes me back to the healer.

"I feel fine," I often remind him. "Please, don't make me drink those awful herbs again."

"I know, but I worry." Samuel scans me head to toe for signs of illness.

After all this time, I should be used to him studying me like I'm a withering flower. But I keep finding myself wanting him to really look at me, not the presumed embodiment of death that's supposed to claim my body but hasn't.

The idea that we won the battle does not go away. Ryan Blacknoc's words of the worms of death fade into ash. I won.

I lift a finger to Samuel's chin. I want him to see me like he saw me in that forest. As horrible as that place was, he looked at me like I could take on a pack of beasts with my feet bound.

Samuel leans in. He presses his lips to mine. I taste him. Embrace him. The world around us shrinks.

****

Grandfather and Samuel sit at the dinner table. My heart warms at the sight of my two favorite men. Samuel passes Grandfather a basket of rolls. I dig into my plate of beef and vegetables as the room soon fills with laughter and chatter. The house is full. Content. I could get used to it.

After dinner, Samuel takes me around the house. Just before sunset, we go on our usual walk into the forest. I fill my lungs with the wooded area. The towering trees stretch up to a sky painted with many colors. Leaves shake to an unheard beat. I pause every so often to take in the flora and the minty grass. The land is truly beautiful when there are no creatures lurking about among the shadows.

"How are you feeling?" Samuel says.

The same question begins to annoy me. He's still on guard for signs of the curse. Why can't he just let it go?

"Alive," I say with a grin.

His hand holds mine. My skirt drags behind on the dirt. As if a kid again, I let go of his hand and sprint off into the distance.

He gains on my heels, and then catches my hand.

I gasp. Laughing, I chase him through the trees. I leap over a fallen log, arms up to protect me from oncoming twigs. Little sun breaks through the tree canopy. Darkness quickly settles on the horizon. Somewhere during my hunt, I lose sight of Samuel. I grin. If I didn't know any better, I would think he has retained his animalistic speed.

I pause and listen. A faint scrape sounds to my right. I circle the area. I slowly close in on the tree I'm eyeing, perfectly confident Samuel is pressed quietly against it.

As I turn the corner to expose the spot, arms wrap around my stomach.

"Gotcha." Samuel kisses the side of my head.

I lean into him, allowing myself to feel his warmth and protective embrace. "Sometimes, I still think the beast remains."

He turns me around, my chest pressed against his. He dips his head, his nose mere inches from mine.

His voice breathy, he says, "Marry me."

****

In the past years of our lives, I've held a permanent position at the tavern as a keeper while Samuel studies to become a coachmaker in Grutchburg City. The jobs help pay for the materials and labor for the house Samuel is building for us not far from Grandfather's house.

I roam the skeleton of our house, my hand grazing over a pole structure that will soon take part in holding a roof over our heads. Two bedrooms. Just like I'd asked for. I make my way to the second bedroom.

"This will be yours little one." I pat the bump in my belly.

It's surreal to think I've been carrying my baby for seven months. I can't wait to see my baby's face, in my arms, in this house. I picture a fence wrapping around the front and back yards much like Grandfather's with chickens and horses. Maybe a few dogs. A garden to feed my family. Grandfather playing with his grandchild. Teaching his grandchild new skills every day. Lost in the vision, I smile like a fool.

Our new family member on the way should make for an interesting challenge caring for a child with one hand but fun, nonetheless. I play with the wedding ring on my left hand. A challenge indeed, but we will make it work.

"Layla."

I jump, turning on my heels. Samuel finds me, leaning in to kiss my cheek. "What are you doing here?"

"You're still sneaking up on me." I pinch his bicep and tiptoe to peck his lips.

"Sorry. I didn't know you would be here."

While rubbing my belly, I say, "How was your visit with your father?"

"Good." Samuel leans against a section of wood frame with arms folded. "He was trying to give us money once again."

I chuckle. "Did you remind him that we can manage?"

"He means well."

"I know." I glance around the house. "How *are* we doing?"

"Progress is slow but forging on." He stares up at the threatening clouds. "I'm afraid no work today. A storm is rolling in, which means you should be home."

I stare up at the gray sky. Storms used to make me anxious, as if they were the cloak of nightfall like those nights in the forest with the monsters. I shove the bygone memories aside, reminding myself how far I've come. The weather is merely an obstacle, delaying us further from completing our house.

"Soon," he says, as if reading my thoughts. "It will

be finished."

****

Grandfather reads as the fire cracks. Rain pelts the windows. Thunder rumbles above us. On the settee, I lean into Samuel's warm side, absorbing every word from the book Mr. Alden loaned us.

When the story finishes, Samuel ushers me to our bedroom. He helps me to bed and tucks me in. I look up at him, smiling. I can see my future in his eyes, our future, the three of us. He kisses my neck. I giggle, pulling him over me. He doesn't put his full weight on me. He rolls on his side of the bed, then turns to face me. His finger traces the bump of my belly. My hand falls over his.

"How are you feeling?" he says.

Samuel learned to stop asking me that question long ago, but now when he asks, I know he means my pregnancy.

I play with his hand. I'm more exhausted than I care to admit.

"Getting through one step at a time," I say.

There must be something in my eyes that tells Samuel I'm not in the mood for conversation because he doesn't say another word, only holds me. I close my eyes. I feel safe in his arms. The pitter-patter of the rain and Samuel's breathing is the perfect melody. Before I know it, I drift into slumber.

Chapter Fifteen

The horror of those days in the cursed forest festers back. During my time as a beast in that horrible place, I thought I'd heard every scream there is to hear, and for a split second I think I'm dreaming, but I'm not. I wake. Layla screams beside me, thrashing and kicking in our bed. She coughs. Coughs again.

Chest pumping up and down, I struggle for our lantern. The light reveals a pale Layla. Dark circles under her eyes mark her. Sweat glistens on her neck and chest. She grows frantic as if searching for a gulp of air.

She shoves herself out of bed, holding her belly. I rush to inspect her for wounds. No signs of injuries on her body. Panic floods me when I realize her injuries may be within her.

"My baby!" she screams.

Layla takes a big step back, slamming against the wall. She hunches, gripping at the sides of her hair. I freeze for a split second, then rush over to her. She teeters, shaking, and nearly falls over. I catch her in my arms. Her entire body shakes with violent tremors.

I hold her close. "Tell me what's wrong. Are you in pain?"

Her wet face grows bright red. Her cheeks are hot. The strain in her voice butches her speech.

"She won!" Layla shrieks like an animal is

chewing off her leg.

The invisible rope around my neck grows taut. “Layla, please—”

She points to something beside the bed. I follow her guidance. There’s a plate-size puddle of black liquid on the wooden floorboards.

“I threw it up,” she says.

I freeze again, now trembling myself. All I can do is hold her. Bile rises at the back of my throat. It can’t be. No. Helplessness builds inside me, buckling the foundation I once called hope. I cry with her, squeezing her in my arms.

Her grandfather rushes into the room, terror filling his face at the sight of us against the wall.

****

My ears still ring from Layla’s screaming. My throat remains raw from all the emotions I tried to keep at bay.

Mr. Marlowe, Layla’s grandfather, closes Layla’s door behind him.

“How is she?” A slight quiver remains in my fingers. I shove them into my pockets.

Mr. Marlowe shakes his head. “I’ve never seen her like this. I fear the worst. It’s the curse, isn’t it? Am I going to lose my granddaughter and grandchild?”

The realization of his question hits me like a wagon of barrels crushing my bones. I must be in a dream because the concept of losing my unborn child and wife seems like a distant ripple that never truly reaches me.

Then, finally, it does. A light in me burns out. The darkest corners of my mind stretch to shadows that quickly cave in my head. My thoughts unravel into a web of anguish that suffocates me. My unborn baby.

My Layla. Am I going to lose my family?

****

Layla doesn't resemble herself until the following week, but she still won't leave her room. With the curse slowly making her ill, she believes any energy she exerts will harm the baby. I exert the energy for her by unleashing it on our house. I spend days hammering. More walls go up. Windows to display the scenery around us installed. Doors to secure our treasures completed. Furniture to provide us comfort assembled.

If she just sees our house, maybe…I don't know what I'm thinking, as if it will somehow help her. But Layla needs to see it finished.

As I make my way back to Layla's grandfather's house, I catch her midwife exiting the room, carrying a chamber pot.

I stop her before she can leave. "Is she eating?"

"She's eating more, yes."

Relief fills me. "That's good news. Thank you."

She nods. "I will continue my prayers for your family."

"Thank you."

I enter Layla's room. The air is stagnant. A crack of light peeks between the drawn curtains. Dead silence causes me to pause. It's almost as if no one occupies the room. I search the bed. Layla has her back to me. Her face points toward the window.

"Layla?"

The second she hears me, she glances over her shoulder and pats the space beside her. "Come, lay with me."

We lay in silence for a moment before Layla finally speaks, her voice laced with sadness I wish I could take away.

"I can't stop…thinking about it. What if my baby is cursed, too? What if he dies?"

I pick up my head to look at her. "He?"

She turns her head to meet my gaze. "Just a feeling."

I place my hand on her belly, worried I'll scratch her with my calloused palms. A strong kick hits the palm of my hand. "He's too strong. He can't possibly be sick. Here."

I move Layla's hand to the spot on her belly where our baby is active.

Layla gasps. "He must know you're here."

Her smile beams, the first one I'd seen in so long. Her concern returns and deepens the lines on her forehead.

"We will have a healthy baby," I say, kissing the side of her head.

"But what if—"

"We can't think such thoughts."

She leans her head on my shoulder, her breathing heavier. I can almost hear the wheels in her mind still turning.

Holding her, I whisper into her ear, "I finished the house."

Chapter Sixteen

Seven years later

Iris skips out of the house. Her hair, as black as Layla's, swings in the breeze. The bright sun highlights the smile spreading on her little face. The bounce in her steps sings the joy she carries for the day. My healthy girl. She blossoms each morning.

Layla once planted the idea of a son. I had expected such but was overwhelmed with joy the moment I locked eyes with my little girl. I'm reminded that Layla isn't always right about everything. Perhaps it's this remainder I cling onto so tightly because I want her to be wrong about her life fading.

Iris pauses at the fence where she scoops up the cat rubbing at her boots.

I call from the threshold, her coat ready in my hand. "Iris?"

She turns with the orange cat cradled in her arms.

"Don't you want to say goodbye to Mommy?"

Her face scrunches in puzzlement. "What for, Daddy? I'm going to see her later."

The knots I've grown accustomed to over the years twist like old gears at the pit of my gut. At seven years of age, Iris is still too young to understand she might not see her mother at any moment, any given day.

"I know but give her one kiss goodbye before we

leave. She loves kisses."

Iris sets the cat down and runs back inside. It must be a quick kiss because she comes running back outside seconds later. I return to Layla and sit on the side of the bed beside her. She lays on her back. Her stomach slowly rises and falls. Nothing can prepare a man for seeing the one he loves in pain. I should be more grateful for Layla that she wasn't bedridden until these last two years, that she was able to spend much of her energy with her family, but I'm not. I want more for her. Layla deserves more than this.

"Layla?" I whisper.

I lean my ear over her mouth. She breathes, barely, as if it's too much effort for her body.

"Layla," I say again. "I'm taking Iris to the library."

Layla's eyes flutter open. She wheezes, as if fingers are crushing her throat. "Yes. She…will like that."

My heart has taken several punctures over the years, and just when I think one more piercing will deflate it, sometimes I wish it would. Even though it saps everything out of me, I rise and stand before her. I can never know if this will be the last time I see her alive. My hand reaches for the blanket and I pull it up to her chin.

Her skin is pale. Her eyes are sunken in. Even her hair has thinned. Her bones pop through her skin. Lumps swell in my throat. I'd give anything to take Layla's place.

I carefully kiss her cheek. "I'll be right back."

"Time," she says. "You…live without…me."

Her words haunt me. She says it with such ease as

if it's no trouble for her.

I shush her. "Please, stop saying that."

She's been saying those words more in the last few weeks. In my heart of hearts, I know she's closer to death's door.

Layla's weak gaze meets mine. "I'm not scared of dying."

"I wish you wouldn't talk about death as if it's a vacation. It takes you away from me, from us, and I can never be fine with that."

"It will be okay. And you and Iris will be okay." She coughs and I rush to hand her a hanky from the nightstand. She continues. "Do you remember the moment you decided life was more important than yielding to what was inside of me?"

I nod. She refers to the day in the woods, when I asked for her hand in marriage, when everything changed for us, except the death living inside her.

"Do you regret it all?" I say.

She pauses, and then smiles. "None."

"Sometimes, I wish you hadn't ended your life for mine."

Her breathing is shallow. "I don't. Because…long ago…a monster gave me something…I didn't deserve. And filled my heart…with more than I could ever imagine."

A creak turns my attention to the door. Iris stands in the threshold. I blink the tears away and force a smile. "Be right there, honey."

****

Iris tugs my hand. "Race you up the steps, Daddy!"

Iris' dark eyes gleam as she slips out of my grasp. She skips a step as she runs up toward the library. She glances back to make sure I'm chasing her. I pursue. I see Layla's strong will rooted deep inside her. It's unmovable like a boulder.

"Hold your horses," I call out with a grin.

My boot catches on a step. I fall on my palms, breaking my fall.

"Daddy!" Iris rushes back to me. Her little hands try to pull me up by my arm. "Are you okay, Daddy?"

My protective nature is locked within her. I peck her cheek and dash by her.

"No fair!" Iris shouts. "That's cheating."

I pivot in time for her to tackle my waist. I lift her. She hugs my neck and points at the building as if telling me to march.

It's hard enough getting her out of the library, and now Mr. Alden encourages her to return for a new book each week. I shouldn't complain. It keeps her mind preoccupied and me full of insight with every new fact she learns from the library.

Iris struggles to pull back the doors of the Grutchburg City Library. I race to help her inside.

Smirking ear to ear, she dashes across the lobby and nearly slams into Mr. Alden's desk.

"What's the rush?" Mr. Alden gazes down at Iris.

"I'm ready to return this." She pulls out the book from her sack and hands it to Mr. Alden. "But…um…I accidentally dropped it in water."

Mr. Alden sighs. "Why am I not surprised?"

I chuckle, reaching across the desk to shake hands with the librarian.

His eyes squeeze into a smile. "Samuel. Always a pleasure."

"Sorry about the book. I'm happy to pay for the

damages."

Mr. Alden holds up a hand. "Not needed. I'll let it slide." He brings his attention back to Iris. "But you better be more careful with those books, young lady."

"Yes, sir!" Iris grins. "I'm going hunting, Daddy."

By hunting, she means finding her next adventure book.

"Okay." I fix her shirt strap back over her shoulder. "I'll be here, pumpkin. Make sure you pick a good one."

She darts off behind rows of bookshelves.

"How are you doing?" Mr. Alden says.

I turn to meet his gaze. "I've been better."

"And Layla?"

My throat thickens. I can't find my words, so I just shake my head.

Mr. Alden swallows. "What about Iris? You still worried about her?"

"Shouldn't I be?" I rub the back of my neck. "I mean, it's been seven years. We've never seen any issues with Iris. Not so much as a winter's cold. But that doesn't stop me from checking on her each night."

"I don't believe you have anything to fear. The curse was broken by Layla's sacrifice. It was her choice. One selfless act by one person."

Nothing makes me want to lash out more than hearing Ryan Blacknoc's words. Any mention of the curse catapults my pulse.

I force a small smile. "Iris still believes her mother will get better. I never know what to tell her. How can I explain to her that her mother will never get better?"

"And you? What do you believe?"

I don't answer him. It no longer matters what I

believe. What I believe will not change what will happen to my wife. I fight back a ball of rage.

"My apologies." Mr. Alden clears his throat. "The last thing I want to do is upset you. Lately, I keep going back to one thing."

"Back to what?"

Mr. Alden leans in. "Can I show you something? It will only take a few minutes."

I glance at Iris, busily scanning the pages of a book.

"Okay."

Mr. Alden leads me down a hall into his study. His desk is free of clutter, with a single black book resting on top. There's no mistaking THE BLACKNOC CURSE written in red on the black leather tome.

Hooves stomp my chest.

"Why are you showing me this?" I snap, my fists balling. "I thought you burned it a long time ago." I'm ready to leave and slam the door behind me, or better yet, burn the room to the ground.

"Wait. Please." Mr. Alden gestures for me to sit. I don't.

"Why didn't you burn the book as I'd asked?" The blood rushing to my head boils.

Mr. Alden hugs the book tighter to his chest. "Because she's still sick. Because I'd hoped I could find something in here." He slaps at the book. "That will cure her."

"The book is nothing but pain and misery. It holds no cure."

"You don't know that. Please, will you just take one last look at it?"

"I won't ask you again to burn it."

"Don't you want to explore all your resources?"

My fingernails dig into my palms. "You know I have."

He lifts the book and gives it a shake like it's a holy book. "But there could be something in here we missed, just like that clue we found that led to your freedom. We wouldn't have spotted it if Layla hadn't tried to burn it. We can't give up on her."

"Don't you say that!" My raised voice startles him. "I have *not* given up on her."

"I know. That's not what I meant. I—"

"Layla won't live much longer, and neither should that damn book. If you won't burn it, I will."

"Layla tried once before, remember? The book doesn't burn."

"No one tried to burn it a second time. Give it to me."

I yank the book out of Mr. Alden's grasp and make my way to the nearest sconce. I toss the book on the stone floor and grab the candle. I shove the candle fire against every corner of the book until the flames start to lick their way toward the center.

Mr. Alden stands without a word, staring at the flames.

The flames completely dance on top of the book. *Pop.* White light engulfs the room, so blinding that covering my eyes with my hands does no good. Even my closed eyelids do no good. A deafening howl of wind smothers my call to Mr. Alden. Heat radiates as if a blazing fire is mere inches from me. I scramble for the door, hoping Mr. Alden follows suit.

A body that I can only assume is Mr. Alden, slams into me, knocking me over. His hands pat my back. I push up and feel for his shoulders for guidance. He latches onto my shoulders. I try to say, "We have to leave," but I can't hear my own words.

Boom! The light flooding the room extinguishes itself. The howling wind stops. A pale Mr. Alden stands directly in front of me. The same questions swirl in his eyes.

"Are you okay?" I ask.

His gaze locks onto something on the floor.

The Blacknoc book. Still intact, on the stone floor.

The blood drains from my face. Mr. Alden rushes to it. He picks it up and flips through the pages.

"Good heavens," he says.

"What is it?"

Mr. Alden's hand wobbles on the back of the book's spine. "It can't be."

"What?" I rush to his side and peek at the page.

My eyes widen. I stare at it as if it'll scorch my hand. A detailed illustration of Layla gazing out the window knocks the breath out of me. Underneath the drawings are paragraphs of Layla's thoughts, her every word with her grandfather, the love she has for him.

I reach for the book and flip through it. More illustrations of Layla and more of her words fill the pages. Paragraphs carry her story that lead up to her meeting me. I see my old monster self as a drawing. I fight for her against the other beasts.

My hands grow clammy.

I nearly forgot Mr. Alden stands in the same room with me. An invisible wave nearly sweeps my feet from under me when I turn to the last page. It reads:

Return to where it began.
Find the place, if you can.

It shines like gold at the first crack of dawn.
Focus on the trunk, to which you are drawn.
Be quick before it all drips.
Perfect and pure only for frail lips.
The blood will take it all away.
Not a speck of death will stay.

A disembodied whisper circles me. "Find it."

I know I'm not the only one to hear it because Mr. Alden gasps beside me. The door behind us slams open. Mr. Alden and I nearly jump out of our skins. Iris stands on the threshold.

She giggles. "What are you two doing here?"

****

After that unfathomable display in the study, I sit across from Mr. Alden near the main foyer of the library, trying to collect myself. My thoughts still spin. The new words of the Blacknoc book tug at my strings of hope, but the threads keep breaking with the idea that the Blacknoc Curse is merely giving me false hope.

Mr. Alden asks, "Are you going to chase this?"

"Whatever *this* is, I can't afford not to." Sweat beads along my head.

Mr. Alden nods, satisfied. "*Return to where it began.* Do you know where that might be?"

I dip my chin, lowering my voice. "I keep thinking about one place. The house of Mara Blacknoc in the Del Rise Mountains. Layla showed me the house long ago. There's nothing there now."

"But what's out there now that could help Layla?"

I shrug. "The book used words like 'trunk' and 'blood.' What could that mean?"

Mr. Alden props his elbows on the table and leans his forehead into his palms. He whispers the poem to himself. For a while, he's silent, then utters, "Tree trunk."

I perk.

His wide gaze meets mine. "The blood of a tree. Tree sap!"

Heads turn our way. I ignore them, realizing we're looking for a tree near Mara Blacknoc's house. That must be it. Has to be.

"But how will we know which tree it is?" I whisper.

"*It shines like gold at the first crack of dawn.* There can't be too many bleeding trees around there."

Chapter Seventeen

I don't waste a second returning home. Layla's grandfather waits at our house, watching over Layla. Iris runs off to play with the cat. After checking on a sleeping Layla, I pull Mr. Marlowe aside into the parlor.

"If I just check it out, maybe it might help," I say, almost pleading.

"Samuel, please." Mr. Marlowe turns his back and folds his arms. "My granddaughter is dying, spending her final moments in our lifetime and you want to leave her side?"

"This could be a real solution. It could cure her. Just listen. *The blood will take it all away. Not a speck of death will stay.* Doesn't that sound specific to the one who ate death? For Layla. This could be it. We have to try."

He turns my way, shaking his head. "You're not leaving her over this foolishness."

"I think you're scared to have hope for her, and you know what, I'm scared too, but I'm going to try everything I can for her."

"And if you don't find what you're looking for, how long will you keep searching before Layla passes on?"

"Once upon a time, Layla didn't give up on me, even when no one believed her, and she stood alone against those beasts."

He drops his head, guilt seemingly flashing across his eyes.

Gritting my teeth, I force myself to utter the words I know he will rebuke. "As long as it takes."

****

When I rush outside to catch a breath, I'm grateful for the unannounced visit from my father. He meets me at the far end of the fence. Father must see the distress on my face because he rushes to hug me. I yank on the back of his collar as I squeeze him, hoping to absorb some shred of his strength.

"What are you doing here?" I finally say.

"I wanted to see how Layla was doing."

I press a heel to the back of my neck. "Not good."

As quickly as I can, I tell my father the latest of what we uncovered. Mixed emotions thicken my tone. Father remains silent. Even if I seem senseless, he knows me well enough to know when to listen without interruptions or judgments.

"It sounds like you know this is something you must do," Father says.

"It is."

"Then do it." Father grips my shoulder. "I'll stay around here until you return."

Relief washes over me. His support somehow adds the stamina I need to put one foot in front of the other.

"Go on." Father gives me a small grin. "Get out of here."

Before I leave, I sit down next to Layla. I won't lie to her about where I'm going. She needs to know what will keep me away.

"I'm doing this for you," I tell her.

She wheezes, each breath so wan I fear it will be her last. "I know I…can't stop you." Her weak hand barely holds onto mine. "But don't…lose yourself…if you don't…succeed."

The words of Layla's grandfather slam back into me. Doubt slithers into my head. Am I a monster for leaving her? This could be her final day, and I'm running off into the woods.

"Samuel." She reaches for me before I go. "Take Iris…with you."

My eyes widen. "I can't do that. It's too dangerous for her."

"With you…it's not." Her words grow faint. "I…don't want her to…see me like this. She's better with you. Please…"

"Okay. Okay." I kiss her cold forehead.

My racing heart nearly knocks the bones out of my chest. Was she bidding us farewell?

****

As soon as we are packed and ready, we load the wagon and set off on the journey. It will take almost a full day to reach the mountains and I have to be in the right location just before sunrise. I pray this quest is not inconsequential.

The wagon bounces over each bump. The hooves of the two horses slow to a calculated pace. The closer we get, the rockier the ride. Iris twists in her seat and digs for something tucked under a sack. She turns around with a bow and quiver in her hands.

I almost jerk the reins. "Where did you get that, young lady? You know you're not supposed to have that. It's too dangerous for a girl your age."

"But, Daddy, Grandfather said I should have it

with me. He said it was okay. He's been showing me how to use it."

I raise a brow at her. "Is that right?" I told him I didn't want her using a bow and he went behind my back. I shake my head.

****

We reach the river. Not too far from here is her house, that witch's house. It feels weird retracing this path back to a place that only brings horrible memories. For one final journey, I hope it leaves a memory that I can look back on with a smile.

The cloak of nightfall quickly casts its net to capture the stars. Crickets orchestrate their songs. The full moon hangs in the sky, spotting our resting area with a silver hue. I help Iris pitch our tent and then gather wood to feed the fire. We sit by the camp, indulging in hot tea and fresh meat I prepared.

Iris refuses to let go of her bow.

"You planning on sleeping with that thing?" I sip from my cup.

The flickering fire lights up her grin. She tilts her chin as she glances at me. "A warrior is never without her weapons."

I chuckle. "Is that so?"

She nods.

Maybe she was reading too many adventure books, or too much of Layla pulsed through her. I give her a sideways hug, forgetting for a moment that we aren't on our usual camping trip.

The nervousness of the two horses tied to the branch catches my attention.

I twist around at the pop of a stick in the brush. Scanning the area, I wait.

Iris breaks my thoughts. "Are the ghosts back?"

Eyes wide, I turn to meet her with a questioning gaze. "What do you know about ghosts?"

She pokes the fire with her stick. "Mommy said there are ghosts in these mountains. I think she still sees them."

"What do you mean?"

"I hear her sometimes when she naps. I think she dreams of ghosts." She reaches into her satchel and pulls out an embroidered pendant of a cross on a leather cord. "I made her one of these. To protect her from the bad ghosts. I made an extra for us, too. To keep us safe."

I grin. "There are no ghosts out here, pumpkin. We've nothing to fear."

I chew on my own words, repeating in my head, Mara is dead. *Layla killed her.*

A snap in the distance startles me to my feet. The noise is closer this time. It's no coincidence. The hooves from my racing heart press into me. I spin on my heels with wild eyes, trying to scan the area, but it's so dark I can hardly tell a shadow from a tree.

"Iris, get inside the wagon and cover your head."

"But why, Daddy?"

"Just do as I say."

My palms grow clammy. I pull my knife from my hip sheath. Just as I am about to turn away, something moves in the brush. A wolf emerges from the tree line. It stares at Iris like it just found a meal for the pack. Slowly, it approaches with lips curled and head dipped.

My thoughts wrestle me. *Mara. Is. Dead.*

I can't shake the idea of Mara having something to do with the animal before me. I stand in front of Iris.

"Get back!" I swing my weapon in the air, trying to seem threatening. "Back!"

The wolf growls and shakes its head violently. Its thick fur gives it an appearance of a mane around its head. Its golden eyes gleam. I stomp my feet and broaden my shoulders. Nothing I do stops the wolf in its tracks. The wolf charges faster, aiming straight at me as if already making up its mind to go through me first.

I grind my boots in the dirt, preparing to fight. My heart pumps faster. My grip tightens around the handle of the knife.

Iris steps out from behind me, bow drawn. She releases the string. An arrow shoots across and stabs into the dirt directly in front of the wolf, stopping it in its tracks.

The wolf stares at the arrow, stunned, almost disoriented. Iris reaches for another arrow in her back quiver, loads her bow, and shoots another. This one penetrates the wolf's paw.

The wolf yelps, turns, and then runs away, back into the trees from where it came.

"I didn't mean to miss the first time, Daddy, but I was scared."

Scanning the area for more, I let out a sigh of relief when no more emerge. I scoop Iris into my arms and kiss the top of her head.

"I was scared too, pumpkin. Thank you. You saved us. My brave girl." How selfish of me to scold her for her interest in archery. I owe her grandfather a huge thanks.

****

I'm too filled with apprehension to sleep. Iris sleeps peacefully in her tent as I sit by the fire. I watch the brush, listening for any signs of wildlife. Howls in the distance add to the bounce in my knee.

Soon, the sun will rise, which means we better make our way to the witch's house. I calculate Iris will loiter behind from lack of sleep, so I'm sure to wake her early and give her enough time to revive. She moans and fights me at first, but then sits upright in her tent like a wide-eyed owl. Somehow, Iris is cheery and ready to take on the rest of the journey. My nerves are still on edge. After that wolf, I almost feel like Mara had a hand in it somehow.

But Mara is dead. It was just an animal like any other animal out here.

I take a deep breath and grip Iris' hand. The path we must take is too dense for our horses and wagon, so we leave them behind until our return.

The woods are quiet. The lantern barely stretches out past three rows of trees. Iris carries her lantern, her bow, and quiver strapped on her back. Her satchel rocks on her hip. My own sack carrying our food and water bounces on my back.

Iris breaks from my grasp and fetches something on the ground.

Iris tugs my shirt. "Look, Daddy, this looks like a troll's face."

She hands me a rock that fits nicely into my palm. I trace my fingers along the cracks and lines that kind of resembles a cranky face.

I hand it back to her. "Keep it."

She tucks it into her satchel and skips in front of me.

"Stay close," I warn.

"Yes, Daddy."

I grin. Her every bounce leads her on her own personal journey.

A rustle of leaves sounds behind me. I whirl, my hand gripping the end of my knife on my hip.

Nothing. I wait but remember Iris.

When I turn back, she's gone. Only my lantern glows.

My heart flees my body.

"Iris?"

I leap forward, checking the nearest tree where I last saw her.

Empty.

"Iris? This isn't a time to play. Please come out this instant."

Dead silence throws my thoughts into a frenzy. I spin around, checking every bush and tree. I even raise my light to the branches.

"Iris!"

Feet spiriting across the foliage turns me in time to catch Iris from tackling my waist.

"Gotcha." She giggles as if we're back in the comfort of our house, but we're not and she fails to realize that. My cheeks grow hot.

"I told you not to wander off."

She shrinks away from my grasp. "But I was playing."

"No," I snap. "You can't do that out here. It's dangerous. Do you not remember that wolf that almost ate us?"

"But I'm not scared anymore, Daddy."

I sigh. "I know you're not, but there could be other animals or things out here intent on hurting us. I can't protect you if you don't stay with me. Do you understand?"

She looks down, slightly nodding her head.

"Good," I say.

I grab her hand and lead us down another trail. Doubt swarms me. Layla's wish or not, I should have left Iris behind. I am a fool for bringing a seven-year-old girl out into the woods.

Chapter Eighteen

Hints of the sunrise bloom above the tree canopy. Any minute, shades of gold and pink will spread across the horizon. A new day awaits, one I can't afford to miss. I must hurry.

Iris tugs my hand as I pick up the pace. Birds chirp their songs from their perches.

"Slow down, Daddy."

I groan, not stopping. "We can't, sweetie. We must be there before the sun rises to see the location of Mommy's special medicine."

She whines. "I can't. I'm too tired."

The poor girl has been dragged out here and hasn't had a decent night's sleep. I am to blame. I scoop her into my arms. My pace grows into a sprint. Iris rests against my shoulder. I steady my hand on the back of her head to keep it from bouncing.

Almost there.

I hop over a fallen log that wasn't there last time I was out here with Layla. The sight almost makes me doubt whether I'm going in the right direction.

Iris snores in my ear. I stop, scanning the area.

"Is this the right way?" I whisper to myself.

My chest quickly rises and falls. A layer of panic begins to peel away. I turn around, eyeing the way I came. The sole of my boot imprints into the soil. Shoving my doubts aside, I turn back to the path and set off.

The wind picks up and shakes the brambles. For a split second, I think I hear a whisper but don't stop to listen. Before I know it, I emerge from the tree line and into the small glade where Mara Blacknoc's house once stood.

The stench of ash that lingered in that place is gone. Fresh dew greets me. I sprint farther into the middle of the glade and spin around. Iris is still sound asleep on my shoulder.

The dark sky grows bluer each minute. Streaks of pink rise higher, along with it, a brilliant sun. It peeks over the tree canopy.

It shines like gold at the first crack of dawn.

My mind spins as I do, looking for anything gleaming from the sun.

"Please," I pray. "Don't let me miss it. Open my eyes."

Focus on the trunk, to which you are drawn.

I slow my turning. Just as I do, a sharp light blinds half my face. I hold my hand out, squinting at the treetops. A brilliant light of orange twinkles.

"That's it!" I shout, waking Iris.

She groans but falls back asleep. I sprint for the tree, nearly tripping on the knee-high weeds. The thrumming in my chest sputters into a frenzy. I reach the tree. The sun lights up the whole area like sparkling diamonds.

And there, gleaming in the ray's path, is the tree sap. I marvel at the droplets shining along the trunk like fireflies. It runs down the trunk from the leaves.

Be quick before it all drips.

I must hurry.

Carefully, I sit Iris down, propping her head against my sack. I pull out my flask and lean it against the trunk under the path of the tree sap.

About a spoonful of drops makes their way into the flask before the tree stops bleeding. The sun moves its finger away from the tree. I look up at the trunk. The drops are gone as if I had imagined them.

"No."

What if what I have is not enough? Familiar panic squeezes my chest. I hurry to cap the flask.

Perfect and pure only for frail lips.

The blood will take it all away.

Not a speck of death will stay.

I pray it will be enough. I must get back to Layla. Scooping up Iris, I head back to our wagon. With the sun lighting the path, I'm able to sprint my way faster to camp.

****

The wagon bounces us higher each time I order the horses to pick up their speed. Iris cries in her seat. She's hungry and can't rest on the rough ride.

"We're almost home."

I want to tell her that I found the medicine that could help Mommy, but I truly don't know if it will help. What if the book's intent is to cause her further harm? Make her death quicker?

I shake my head, half wanting to slam it against the floorboard. If I truly believed that, I wouldn't have gone this far to collect the sap for her. It will work. It must.

The strength of the horses carries us home. Relief lifts my heavy arms when I recognize our fence. That relief washes away when I spot Father slouched by the barn. The weight of the world looks like it hangs around his neck.

What is wrong?

As I stop the horses, Father collects himself, then rushes toward the wagon. He reaches for Iris, picking her up out of the wagon and setting her down.

"There's my favorite granddaughter." His tone sympathetic and breaking with tears. "Where is this new kitty of yours?"

I shoot him a questioning gaze. He gives me a troubled look as if to go along with it. His eyes are bright red.

Father coughs, holding onto Iris' hand. "Come on, honey, show me where."

"I have the sap," I say to Father.

He looks down, shaking his head. Then he leads Iris toward the barn.

No. My brain fogs. I leap off the wagon and sprint inside. Each step I take drives spears through every inch of my body. My throat seals shut. My eyes dry from disbelief.

Just as I pass over the threshold, hands press against my shoulders, stopping me in my tracks.

Mr. Marlowe stands before me. His eyes are red, too.

His voice cracks. "Samuel—"

"No!" I shove his hands away.

"If you'd just been here a few minutes ago, you could have said goodbye." Anger begins to swell his tone.

"No. She can't be."

"She's gone."

"No. I have the cure. I have it!" I yank off the flask

hanging from my neck.

"She's dead now, damn it!"

I ignore him and rush past him. The door to our bedroom is closed. I shove it open.

An unbreathing Layla lays in the bed. Her hands neatly tucked on top of her chest. I rush to her, dropping to my knees. My hand reaches for her cheek. It's cold.

"No. Layla." Tears burst out from my eyes. "Layla, I found it."

She doesn't respond. I lower my ear to her nose. The bottom of my ear touches her cold lip.

Perfect and pure only for frail lips.

The blood will take it all away.

Not a speck of death will stay.

It will work! I yank the cap off the flask and press the end of the flask to her lips. I tilt the flask until every drop of sap is inside her. Then I close her lips and tilt her chin back.

"Layla?"

Dead silence pushes me further to my knees where I crumble. A thousand lashes tear open my heart, bleeding me dry. An invisible hand reaches inside me and takes something of mine I never knew could be taken. My spirit bends under the weight of endless pain. Blow after blow, something snaps in me. I grip the edge of the sheets, screaming into them until my throat peels raw.

"Samuel?" a soft voice says.

I look up with swollen eyes, my gaze hazy.

I melt further into the ground, remembering this is the same beautiful woman I fell in love with back in those woods. Earthy brown eyes stare back at me. The beautiful color of her dark skin has return to health. Her brows are rich. Her long black hair, thick and full.

My disbelief forces me to reach for her hair. The silky strands slide between my fingers. Then I touch her cheek. Warmth spreads into my palm.

I inch closer to her lips and cup her face.

“Layla? It’s really you?” My voice is hoarse.

“It is.”

Her hand grips my arm and she rests her forehead against mine, our noses barely touching.

Her lips part as she stares deep into my eyes. “How?”

“From the book. Tree sap. I—” I choke on my words. “Layla, I thought I lost you.”

Tears spring back as I remember her motionless body. The grip of death claiming her body.

Her strong arm wraps around my neck. “No. I’m here now.”

We hold each for a moment longer before she pulls away.

“Iris?” Layla says.

I clean my face and fetch our daughter and everyone else. Iris screams in cheer at her mother’s appearance. It’s hard to not notice the difference when the effects of the worms are no longer present.

“Did Daddy’s medicine help you?”

“It did, sweetie,” Layla said, holding Iris in her lap and showering her with kisses. “And I heard you helped, too.”

“I did. I even shot a wolf.”

Layla glances at me with a questioning gaze. Grinning, I shake my head. I’ll have to explain later.

Mr. Marlowe and Father crowd the room too,

taking in Layla's lively appearance. Father shakes my hand and gives me a bear hug. Layla's grandfather is speechless and eyes his granddaughter as if any minute she'll disappear.

Chapter Nineteen

Three years later

Every breath I take I am grateful for. For so many years, I truly believed I was meant to die. So much so, that I had accepted it. But Samuel refused to let me go. I could never repay him. I don't deserve a man like Samuel.

There were days I doubted our miracle was true. I feared maybe the tree sap wouldn't be enough and one day the worm's toxin would somehow come back to finish me off, but once again I live by faith and continue life with my family.

The moment I could rest my fluttering heart was when Mr. Alden claimed that one night the book ignited on its own. Burnt to ash. Gone. Forgotten, as if its purpose was lost to the world. With that, I knew I was completely free. We were free from it all. Samuel. Me. Iris. We could live in peace.

Sitting on the bench next to Samuel, I take in the morning air.

His fingers intertwine with mine.

Iris plays with her friends by the meadow, not far from our house. Their giggles and shouting reach us. Grandfather, Samuel's father, and the labor workers help to add another room to our house.

I grin, leaning against Samuel's shoulder.

Samuel moves his hand to the bump in my belly. He brings his lips close and presses them against mine.

A word about the author…

Tori V. Rainn was born and raised in Texas. In her late teens, she became a writer in 2011 when she took a writer's course at Writer's Village University.

If she's not working on novellas or novels, she can easily be distracted with coming up with her next big short story adventure. Several of her short stories have been featured in online magazines.

When she's not writing, she enjoys knife collecting and running. Tea and chocolate are her addictions. Video games, books, music, and movies are her outlet. She's a Christ follower and Realm Makers member.

Visit her at:

https://torivrainn.wordpress.com/

Thank you for purchasing
this publication of The Wild Rose Press, Inc.

For questions or more information
contact us at
info@thewildrosepress.com.

The Wild Rose Press, Inc.
www.thewildrosepress.com

www.ingramcontent.com/pod-product-compliance
Lightning Source LLC
Chambersburg PA
CBHW071943170626
46813CB00005B/1808